SURVIVAL FOR THREE

NICOLE STEWART

STAY INFORMED ABOUT NEW RELEASES FROM NICOLE STEWART!

Visit the link below to **sign up to get list exclusive discounts, news about new releases, and the opportunity to be a VIP reviewer and get all my books for FREE for life!**

http://beechwoodpublishing.com/nicolestewartfans

I promise that this is not a spam list.

PROLOGUE

T he car explosion shook the earth beneath Lincoln Easley's feet. "I hated that Beamer anyway," he quipped as he took off running. A musical score played in his head—the way it always did when his ass was on the line—something punchy and suspenseful. Horns. Lots of horns.

Bullets whizzed by. He dove to the ground and yanked his last remaining gun from his shoulder holster. Ignoring the gravel and oil stains that were wrecking his new tuxedo, he flipped on his back and returned fire as he scrambled under a truck for cover. Too late, his target darted for cover too. Lincoln sucked his teeth. "Gotta be quicker than that next time."

When he heard a muffled sob behind him, he reflexively aimed in that direction. There was a young family hiding under the SUV with him. Dad, mom and a toddler. Innocent civilians. Lincoln's expressive face telegraphed dismay. "Just what I need," he growled.

"Please! Don't hurt us!"

"Shh!" Lincoln put a finger to his lips to silence the scared woman.

"You!" an officer shouted. "Check that alley! You two, come with me!"

Lincoln was a covert agent tasked with assassinating a diplomat accused of espionage. He had planned to do exactly that, until he stumbled upon a sordid tale of sex, money and power. Someone in Washington wanted his target dead for personal reasons—and politicians with hurt feelings could start wars.

Lincoln made a judgement call to fall back and wait for further intel, which angered someone high up. Now he had friends *and* enemies after him with a burn notice that accused him of being a terrorist. He had no clue who was behind any of it, and with the odds stacked against him, Lincoln doubted his chances of making it out of this thing alive.

He held his breath as a squad of men sprinted past the vehicle where he was hiding. They looked like police, but Lincoln wasn't sure of anything anymore. The security guard who had chased him this far was certainly not who he had seemed to be. Besides, not even the good guys would show him mercy if they thought he was a terror suspect.

"Where's a friend when you need one?" Lincoln gritted his teeth in frustration, knowing he could nix the thought of the intelligence community coming to his aid. He glanced at the young family hiding with him. They were a liability. He wanted to leave them, but he was torn between his training and his upbringing. What would his mother think of the man he had become?

Lincoln closed his eyes and let out a breath. He had to take them with him. A stray bullet could be deadly. He wanted no more innocent blood on his hands. "I'm not gonna hurt you. I'm gonna get you out of here," he promised quietly. He beckoned for the trio to follow his lead. At that moment, the toddler whimpered.

One of the officers raced back. "Hey, I think I heard something!" he shouted.

When the portly man hunched down with his weapon unwittingly pointed at the baby, Lincoln hit him hard in the face with the butt of his gun. He quickly threw a flash-bang grenade to the middle of the street to buy them time.

Another deafening explosion filled the air with sparks and smoke, and Lincoln rolled from beneath the SUV. "Let's go! We have to move!" He and his charges sprinted down an alley to where he had stashed his other car.

"Where are you taking us?" The young man huffed, trying to keep up with the toddler in his arms, and a look of guilt flitted over Lincoln's face. Without even trying to, he now had hostages. *I'll look like the bad guy to the very end*, he thought.

"Someplace safe," Lincoln hedged.

He knew the script. The young man would be killed. The young woman would turn to Lincoln to keep her and her child safe. Passion would ignite in this heart-tugging, action-packed spy thriller with a hint of romance. It was exactly the kind of character he loved to play.

Suddenly, the main camera whizzed along a suspension cable for a close-up of their faces as they made it to the luxury car, and the boom stick was whisked out of the frame. Lincoln slowed his pace, knowing camera angles would make him look as if he was running much faster than he was.

"And...cut!" the director yelled.

"Finally!" Lincoln gasped.

The set came alive with activity. People on the sidelines burst into action to take care of the talent. Someone raced forward with a towel and patted Lincoln's forehead and he grimaced at the unnecessary attention.

"Careful not to smudge his makeup!" the scriptie warned.

Lincoln shrugged away from the helping hands and wove through the crowded set to the video village where his buddy Mitch Trepan, the director, stared at the monitor. "How did I do, Mitch? Do we need another?" Christ, he hoped not.

"We're losing light," the camera assistant informed them. Mitch looked to the Director of Photography who nodded in agreement. Frowning, Lincoln glanced at the footage. Mitch was acting like they needed another take. Lincoln's insecurities flared like a bad case of gout, but the director clapped him on the shoulder reassuringly.

"Nah! The guys in accounting will kill me if I squeeze in more pyrotechnics," Mitch laughed, "and Suki will join the mob if I don't get back to the hotel soon. That's a wrap for today. You were fantastic, Lincoln. Nobody but you could have pulled that off."

"Well, it was a team effort," Lincoln replied modestly.

Mitch rolled his eyes. "Don't give me that. You're part of the team. I see you! So much growth from the young man I met years ago. Anyway, tomorrow we film the final scene. I'm itching to start something new. Did you get a chance to read that script I sent to your trailer?"

"Oh, yeah!" Lincoln fibbed. "I loved it!" He knew he *would* love it when he finally got the time to read it. Lincoln's life was a blur of filming, interviews and appearances. He barely had time to shower, much less put his feet up with a good screenplay.

"Landon Ashville delivered the perfect role for you. Make time in your schedule for a new project, if you can. I, uh...I just have one request." The director ushered Lincoln away for privacy and gave him a piercing look that made him a little uneasy.

"Anything you need."

"I want you to take," said Mitch, "some additional training—a survival course—to prepare for a role of that magnitude."

Lincoln laughed in surprise. "You want me to take a survival course?"

"Don't sound so put out. We're not talking our usual Mitch Trepan/Lincoln Easley production. This is a major man versus nature film. Now, you do amazing in urban settings, but it's a lot of character to carry. You think you can handle it?"

"You make it sound like you have doubts."

Mitch shrugged. "I know the extra training will take your innate ability to the next level." He pulled a pamphlet from his pocket and pressed it to Lincoln's chest, backing toward the set. "I'll see you tomorrow morning, bright and early to finish up. *Vengeance with a Vengeance* is going to be huge, I can just feel it. Anyway, take a look at that brochure and give it some thought."

"Thanks, Mitch. See you tomorrow." Lincoln pocketed the brochure and grunted noncommittally as he made his way to his trailer. He was supposed to stop at wardrobe to get out of his clothes, but he needed a breather. Unfortunately, someone called his name, and he looked back to see one of the supporting cast making a beeline for him. "What's up, Carmen?"

"You remembered my name!" she gushed. "Most of the rest of the cast don't. I'm just 'that girl from TV' to them. Um, me and a few friends are going to a local club tonight. Care to join us?"

Lincoln wrinkled his nose. "Eh, I was planning to change and head back to the hotel. I'm not one for big crowds."

"Let's keep it personal, then. You and me." She arched a brow and moved closer, but Lincoln unconsciously put some distance between them. Her flirty smile turned sheepish. "Or, not. Maybe I'm not your type."

"Don't be ridiculous!" he laughed. "I don't have a type."

"Yeah, no! I get it. You're sexy, talented and famous. Of course, you're playing the field! Gosh, I'm so embarrassed that I let my friends talk me into thinking I stood a chance. It's just that I'm getting over a break up with this jerk who turned out to be dating someone else, and…" She laughed nervously. "Just do me a favor. Don't tell anyone I came onto you. I'd rather they not know I've made a fool of myself. *Again.*" She rolled her eyes.

"Hey! Nothing to be embarrassed about. To be honest, I'm flattered."

Her blush faded as he made her feel at ease. "Thanks for being a good sport about this."

"No problem. It's been a pleasure working with you, Carmen. I hope you and your friends have a fun time tonight. Now, if you'll excuse me…" Lincoln slipped into his trailer with a sigh of relief. He did not know which was more taxing, the acting for the cameras or keeping up appearances on the other side of the lens. No one knew how hard he worked to project self-assurance. Especially when he was not feeling particularly self-assured.

People like Carmen thought he had everything—sex appeal, fame, unshakeable confidence—but Lincoln was more than aware of his shortcomings. He peered at the glossy brochure. "Survive Anything," he muttered to himself. "The role is perfect for me, but I need extra training. Go figure. They ought to teach how to survive Hollywood."

~

A few thousand miles away, Nadia Marson hunkered down with the other upmarket guests at a luxury resort. She had never been so terrified in her life. Her heart slammed in her chest at the shrieking and howling wind, and she squeezed her eyes shut and sent up a quick prayer.

Mr. Man Upstairs, I know we don't talk much, but if I get out of this alive, I swear I'll get help for my chocolate addiction, she promised. *I'll even give up my love affair with strappy heels!*

Nadia loved the good life, but she would give up anything to make it through this storm. She had paid a fortune for a private getaway to sip piña coladas with hot, bare-chested men. The island she had chosen to visit was supposedly one of the safe ones. The travel agency had assured her that the climate was benign.

So, when the bad weather warning was issued the prior evening, Nadia had not worried. Forecasters predicted the storm would veer and the resort would avoid a direct hit. But Mother Nature had different plans and Nadia was now stuck in the middle of a category three hurricane.

"Everybody, stay calm!" a hotel staff member yelled. His expression looked as panicked as Nadia felt. Thunder boomed, and the handful of guests in the hallway let out a collective yelp. The entire hotel shuddered and heaved. Then, the power went out. The only illumination came from purple and cobalt clouds and white rain seen through the picture windows of the lobby

How can anyone stay calm in this? Nadia chanced a peek at the storm. Wind-whipped palm trees flailed helplessly as the relentless rain lashed the building. But that was not the worst of it. She squinted to make sure she was seeing what she thought she was seeing: a wall of water rising in the distance.

"Oh, my God!" Nadia gasped.

"The storm surge! Everybody get upstairs!" someone ordered.

The ocean climbed higher as it raced toward the hotel. Others ran, but Nadia was paralyzed by fear. The giant wave crashed through the gilded doors of the lobby with a deafening boom. Gusts of wind swept her raven hair around her pale, startled face and a particularly strong one knocked her to the floor.

As hotel furniture was smashed into driftwood, Nadia scrambled away, trying to climb to her feet, but failing. Her wild eyes took in the water rushing toward her. *I'm gonna die*, she thought. She braced herself for impact.

She squeezed her eyes shut, and she saw everything she had come to the islands to escape: The lavish lifestyle she had left behind to take a breather in paradise, the pressures of being an heiress to a multi-billion-dollar megacorporation, not to mention the failed relationship with her ex-boyfriend.

Damn you, Jason Stratham! This was his fault. If the social-climbing playboy had not cheated on her with that vapid reality TV show star, she would be home in Texas. Nadia fled the states because her name was dragged through the mud when the tabloids discovered that Jason was two-timing her.

She was Nadia Pamela Marson, the sole heiress of wealthy oil magnate Wilson Marson, and consequently the media was having a field day taking her down several notches. Her father was grooming her to take a position within the company, an idea that held no appeal to her at all.

"*Señorita! Dios mio*, come quickly!" A housekeeper grabbed Nadia's hand and yanked her from the floor. Nadia recognized her; she was the girl who patiently listened to her problems every morning while tidying up her hotel room. "You have to move, *señorita!* We have to go!"

"Go where? The water is everywhere!" Nadia cried.

"Just follow me!"

She clung to the woman's hand and ran behind her. They were the last up the stairs and the ocean swiftly rising around them. The hotel groaned and complained, but, amazingly, it held. Finally, they reached the top floor where thirty or forty guests and staff members were crowded in the hall.

Nadia breathlessly moved to the banister to stare down at the angry water swirling to the second story. As quickly as it had come, it was receding. But before she could breathe a sigh of relief, she overheard a manager discussing the dire situation with a cluster of hotel employees. The whispered exchange brought up a question of whether there would be enough food. The emergency generators were out, and rescue might be several days away.

Nadia looked around to see if anyone else heard the conversation. The others looked too overcome by what they had been through to even think about what was ahead. None of them—including Nadia—looked equipped for a hard couple of days with limited food and water, along with no power.

Nadia bit back a sob and yanked her cellphone out of her oversized handbag. "Damn it!" she swore as she realized service was down. There would be no calls for a helicopter or a private plane. What pilot in his right mind would travel in a hurricane, anyway? Worst of all, she could not call her father to let him know what was happening.

I'm sorry, Dad, she thought helplessly. She knew what Wilson Marson would say to that. *Don't be sorry. Be better.* There was nothing she could do to make up for leaving home without telling her family where she was going, but she could at least be of service here.

Nadia wiped her tears as she approached the young housekeeper who had forced her into action. Smiling tremulously, Nadia read her name tag, something she ruefully realized she had not done at any other point during her stay.

"Maria, you saved my life. I…I can't thank you enough," she sniffed. Maria's eyes widened in surprise when Nadia impulsively pulled her into a tight hug. It felt good to lend comfort and be comforted.

Maria gently disengaged with tears in her eyes, as well, as she looked around at the shaken guests. "I am so sorry you all have to go through this, *señorita*," said the housekeeper.

"Well, we're all in this together, right?" Nadia tried to laugh.

"The storm will be over soon," Maria assured her.

Nadia glanced at the window at the end of the hallway. Indeed, the storm seemed to be losing strength but the damage had been done. The resort town was devastated by the storm surge for as far as the eye could see. The few remaining buildings speared from the ocean. No land was in sight. Nadia choked up as understanding dawned that there were people who would not live to tell this tale.

"Do you have family members out there?" she gasped.

"Mi madre is working here at the hotel with me. It's just the two of us."

"Oh, thank goodness!" she breathed a sigh of relief. "I want to help. I can't just stand around, waiting for things to get worse. What can I do?" Before Maria could turn down her offer, Nadia grabbed a stack of blankets from one of the staff members in passing.

She delivered the warm throws to guests and offered words of encouragement as someone else unlocked a vending machine and handed out snacks and sodas.

No one mentioned how long they would be forced to stay in the dank, lightless hotel or when the hotel rations would be exhausted. Nadia decided she would keep busy until her time was up or until she heard helicopter blades cutting through the air, signaling that they were saved. Whichever came first.

But if she got out, she would do whatever was necessary to never be this helpless again.

CHAPTER 1

Perry Evans bounded into the hangar with extra pep in his step, grateful to be back in business. After months of a slump in business, he was on his way to meet new students. Their plane would be arriving any second and that meant money in the bank. He could finally make some repairs at the cabin so old man Clyde could stop worrying about the upcoming winter.

But Perry's good mood evaporated when he glanced up and realized that his competitor, the owner of Empowered Survival, had beat him to the private airfield. "Rick Feldman," he sighed.

"Perry! Got a class coming in, too?"

"I do. Didn't expect to see you here, though." *I would have re-scheduled*, Perry thought.

"Oh, you know how I am. I like to stay busy!" Rick clapped him heartily on the back and managed to hit his injured shoulder. Perry was sure that it was no accident, but he schooled his face not to show his pain. Perry stepped away and surveyed his rival, trying to figure out why Rick had traded in his faux Native American look for the fatigues of a second-rate drill sergeant.

"Nice get-up," he grunted in amusement.

"The fatigues? Yeah, I took what you did and went one better,"

Rick bragged. "I can't say I'm a former Navy SEAL, but I can look the part."

"Interesting. I guess it helps. Even Boy Scouts wear uniforms."

"Hardy-har-har," Rick smirked.

Perry hid a smile. "Do you give out merit badges, too?"

"Keep the jokes coming while I laugh all the way to the bank. I've been doing this ten years, and the classes just get bigger and bigger. Speaking of which, how's your growth this quarter?"

Perry bit his tongue to keep from pointing out he taught a *real* survival course, as opposed to a glorified spa retreat. Rick Feldman advertised kumbayas around campfires. People had to be serious about learning bush-craft to sign-up for Perry's three-week Survive Anything course. "Business is picking up."

"Well, yeah! Anytime there's uncertainty in the world, business booms," Rick said. "Gotta love the spoiled, scared millennials. Am I right? I tell my students that, with the right training and preparation, they can survive whatever life throws at them. But you and I know better. In any given situation, survival is ninety percent luck."

"If you say so." Perry watched the first plane swoop down and ease into the hangar. He met Rick Feldman's smug gaze and spoke over the noise. "Training and preparation kept me out of a lot of scrapes. In my experience, survival is ninety percent readiness, and ten percent luck."

Rick snickered and pointed at the passengers debarking. "I think this one is yours. And, I gotta tell you, I don't know if you're prepared to deal with *that*. But good luck, buddy." As Perry looked to see what he was talking about, Rick patted his bad shoulder again.

The first passenger off the small plane was a stylishly dressed man with thick, wavy hair and a face made for magazines and movies. He haughtily twirled his fingers for the pilot to grab his luggage as he gabbed away on his cellphone and ambled down the stairs without watching where he was going. A forklift nearly drove into him and Perry suppressed a groan.

The second passenger was no better. She tossed long black hair over her shoulder and slid designer shades to her face as she clutched an oversized purse and daintily made her way out of the plane. She looked flawless in a pastel pink business suit that emphasized her curvy figure. She was a looker, but Perry's spirits just sank even further.

To add insult to injury, he noticed Rick walking out to meet the other plane, a much bigger transport loaded with new students. Perry was still teaching one or two people at a time while Rick's classes grew "bigger and bigger." Rubbing the bridge of his nose, Perry squared his shoulders and confronted his unsuitable enrollees.

"No cellphones," he growled as he snatched the phone from passenger one and dumped it in the nearest wastebasket.

"Dude! What the fuck? That's an eight-hundred-dollar phone!"

"And the rules were in the contract you signed and agreed to. No cellphones or computers or electronic devices of any kind. I specifically stated any contraband would be confiscated."

"And destroyed?" Tall, dark and handsome looked incredulous.

Perry swung his gaze from him to the woman. "Also, I specified what students were to wear. Right down to the socks and shoes. You need thermals, loose pants—"

"I have mine! I have everything you specified in my bags, plus a few extra ensembles—like this little number—for our days off." The chirpy female waved and smiled vibrantly.

"There are no days off," Perry stated flatly, feeling his patience wearing thin.

"Oh." She looked surprised. "Um, okay. I'm Nadia Marson, and you are?"

Perry stared at her feet. "Wait a second. Are those…Christian Louboutins?"

"They are! Who would guess a man like you would know fashion! They're fab, aren't they?"

Perry dropped his head in his hand. "Take them off."

"I beg your pardon?"

"Take. Them. Off." As she hastily slipped off her shoes, he pulled his notepad from his back pocket to see what he was dealing with, here. "Alright, Nadia and Lincoln, right?"

"That's right. I'm *the* Lincoln Easley from Hollywood," Lincoln bristled.

"Congratulations! I'm *the* Perry Evans from around the way. I'm your instructor, and your first lesson will be in following directions. Please go through your bags and remove only the approved belongings that you will need for your three-week stay. Make arrangements for the rest of your luggage to be shipped back or deposit it in the dumpsters behind the building."

"Excuse me?" Lincoln crossed his arms defiantly.

"Your second lesson," said Perry firmly, "will be in affording me the respect I demand. Don't question me. Don't hold me up. Just do what the fuck I tell you to do, and I'll teach you how to survive anything. Are we clear?"

Lincoln and Nadia shared a look. Nadia was the first to recover. She frowned with displeasure but nodded. "Crystal," she whispered.

Perry finally smiled. "Good. When you're done dumping your luggage, meet me at the front of the building for your only hotel stay of the trip. Tomorrow morning, we go into the woods. If you want to back out, now is your chance." He gestured at the plane that was refueling to leave. This was shaping up to be the one instance that Perry wished his students would cancel.

Nadia slammed the door to her upgraded hotel suite and paced the room. "Ugh! He's impossible! What the fuck have I signed up for?" she raged. She wanted to show Perry Evans she did not need him, but back home her father was prepping her for a job she abhorred. If she returned now, it would signal that she was ready for hire.

Nadia was stuck between a rock and a hard place. She knew Wilson Marson had only stepped up his efforts to give her a job to help her get over any lingering feelings for Jason Stratham. Not that there were any but there was no way to tell her dad that. After six months of living single, she needed to get laid more than she needed any nine-to-five.

She had vowed to learn survival skills ever since the hurricane, but there had to be other training courses besides Survive Anything. She did not have to stay *here* to avoid her father. Nadia sat up and reached for her cellphone to find a new vacation spot. Then, she remembered Perry had confiscated her phone and her iPad.

Plus, all her luggage was gone. She could not believe that arrogant son of a bitch had forced her to give up her belongings. She hated to think of herself as spoiled, but how was she to make it without her beautiful shoes?

In the meantime, she had to check in with her dad. She picked up the hotel phone and reluctantly called him, tapping her Louboutin against the footboard as she waited for the line to connect. When Wilson answered, her heart skipped a beat.

"D-dad!" Nadia cleared her throat and erased the nervousness from her voice. "How's it going?"

"It would be much better if I could get my little girl to come to her senses," he said dryly.

She held in a sigh. *No*, she thought. *I'm not giving up that easily.* "Uh, my flight arrived okay, and I've met the instructor. He's...challenging, but well-qualified. He's a former Navy SEAL, and I think he'll be able to teach me everything I need to know so I won't meet another hurricane unprepared."

"I can't believe I nearly lost you in that storm, but it all could have been avoided, Nadia. You never should have been on that island in the first place. You were supposed to be here. I had training seminars lined up for you so imagine my surprise when I learned you had gone on vacation."

"Can we put that behind us, Dad? Look, I'm sorry I didn't tell you about the getaway. I needed time to think, and I couldn't do that at home. Look, nobody expected that storm to hit the island and—" Nadia realized her tone was becoming increasingly defensive. She shook her head and bit her bottom lip. "I don't want to fight. I simply called to tell you I'm settled at the hotel. I didn't want you to worry."

"Well, I do worry," Wilson said gruffly. "Marson Oil and Gas needs you. I need you."

"I know, Dad," she whispered. "But we've been over this a thousand times. I'm not sure I'm cut out for the work you want me to do. I can't say for certain that I'd take the job, if you offered it to me."

"When I find the right position for you, you'll come around to it. A Marson always rises to the occasion."

"But what if I don't want to rise to the occasion? What if I don't agree with what you're doing? What if I genuinely think you're destroying the planet?"

"You and I both know it's not that cut and dried," he said quietly. "I know what this is really about. You're scared Nadia, you feel like you're not ready for so much responsibility, but you are ready for this, sweetheart. Besides, it'll help you get over that nasty business with Jason."

"You mean it'll give the press something else to talk about."

"That, too," he acknowledged.

Nadia rolled her eyes and suppressed a sigh. It was pointless to argue with her father. He always got his way, whether right or wrong. He saw her reluctance as mere self-doubt but she had serious ethical concerns about the oil and gas industry. The more he pressed her to work for the family business, the less she wanted to be a part of it.

"I'll keep what you've said in mind, Dad, but I have to go. I need to get some rest."

Nadia ended the call and stared blankly into space. At least she had a few weeks to decide how to handle her dad, even if it meant putting up with her arrogant instructor. She wanted to talk to her now-best friend, Maria, about the shitty welcome party.

In the six months since the hurricane, Nadia and the housekeeper from the storm-ravaged resort had become inseparable. She had convinced Maria to get a student visa and come to America to study hospitality. Now, they chatted every day. Maria always gave it to her straight, and Nadia appreciated her candor. She was the only person she trusted with her deepest secrets.

Unfortunately, the dictatorial Perry had effectively cut her off from her best friend; Maria's number was stored in her cellphone. Nadia started to pout until she remembered her assistant had access to her contacts. She grabbed the hotel phone again. "Hi! It's me. Can you patch me through to Maria? I don't have my cellphone."

"Right away, Ms. Marson."

She paced the room, waiting to hear Maria's voice. Instead, she got her voicemail. Nadia groaned and smacked her forehead. "Damn it! I forgot you were in class. Just FYI, I'll be out of touch for the next few weeks. The instructor guy was serious about no cellphones. When in the woods, do as the woodlanders, I guess. I'll...write?" she chuckled. "I'll find a way to keep you posted about my misadventures with two hotties in the wilderness."

She hung up the phone and stretched out in bed with time to kill. It was late Sunday morning. She had a whole day ahead of her, which, she imagined, was to give students ample opportunity to figure out that Perry Evans was a nightmare. She wondered what her bubbly bestie would have to say about his insufferable ultimatum to respect him or hit the tarmac.

Nadia giggled, knowing exactly what Maria would say if she saw him. Respect the man!

Perry was gorgeous, with his cool blue gaze and five o'clock shadow. He had a face that was easy on the eyes, and a body that begged to be touched. With six months of celibacy under her belt, Nadia desperately wanted to touch *something*. Too bad he was a total dick.

Lincoln Easley was just as sexy, but he was full of himself. He was also Hollywood. After her experience with Jason and the reality star mistress, Nadia had lost interest in the false glamour of Hollywood celebrities.

But she could not deny her attraction to both Lincoln and Perry. How would she survive three weeks alone in the woods with men like them?

∼

17

L incoln settled in the chaise lounge by the window with the new script in one hand and a mug of hot tea in the other. Perry had tried to rattle him, but he refused to let the man get under his skin. There would be no running back to LA without giving Survive Anything his best shot. Hence the tea and screenplay. Lincoln desperately needed to achieve equilibrium before dealing with Major Asshole again.

Sunlight poured through the blinds and warmed his face, a subtle sign from nature that—regardless of his mood or melancholy—he was where he was supposed to be. *In an over-priced boutique motel with two caricatures,* Lincoln thought wryly. *The spoiled brat temptress and the overcompensating G.I. Joe.*

Lincoln felt a twist of regret that Mitch Trepan thought he needed this survival course in the first place. He was an established actor with a resume a mile long, and at twenty-seven, he was in his prime. So, what was it about the screenplay that made the director think he should spend three weeks in the wilderness preparing for it?

Lincoln flipped open the manuscript and started reading. The opening scene came alive in his mind. He absently sipped his cooling tea while the story took shape, but gradually the enthralling plot made him forget the tea.

He paid no attention to time ticking away. He did not even notice the room getting darker as evening fell. He was half-way through his copy when he slammed it shut and looked around the hotel room blankly, coming back to reality.

"This is it," he whispered. "This is my career-defining role." He launched from the chaise lounge and paced, knowing that he looked like a madman, but he could not contain his excitement. "This is it!" He laughed.

He saw his name on the screen for best actor. He envisioned the awards and plaques that would line his mantelpiece after this. He grabbed the screenplay and shook it in amazement. It was unlike any other role he had ever played, but Mitch was right, Lincoln thought soberly. No matter how much he hated being stuck on Nowhere

Mountain, he needed the survival training to give him the edge that he was going to need.

With that in mind, Lincoln forced himself to sit and calm down. It was not time to celebrate yet. Not until he completed the course. He turned the television on. He would finish reading the rest of the screenplay some other time, when he could focus on it and not on whatever trials lay ahead on this glorified camping trip. Lincoln sat up when realized the entertainment news segment was on. He turned up the volume. It was one of his favorite shows.

"Looking for the next big blockbuster hit?" the entertainment newscaster asked excitedly. "Rumor has it, director Mitch Trepan is ready to deliver! We caught up with him on the red carpet to get the inside scoop, and here's what he had to say."

Lincoln grinned as his buddy filled the screen. Mitch was at an awards ceremony that Lincoln had missed, but he would be there next year. "Best Actor…Imagine that," he whispered to himself.

"Mr. Trepan, we know you just finished working on *Vengeance with a Vengeance*, but can you tell us what's coming next?" asked the reporter.

Mitch smiled and nodded at the camera. "Get ready for action like you wouldn't believe! That's all I can tell you." He laughed.

"That's your signature," the reporter laughed along. "We know you deliver great action, great heroes. Any ideas for your next film? Give us something. Give us anything!"

"Landon Ashville, who wrote *Well-worn Suicide Note* for me, has delivered a tremendous new script. We'll begin work on it very, very soon."

"Any hints on who we might see in the new picture?" The reporter jabbed the microphone at Mitch again, and the director chuckled good-naturedly.

"Lincoln Easley and I have talked about the role. He did fantastic in *Vengeance with a Vengeance*," said Mitch.

Lincoln warmed with pleasure at the shout out. No matter how many years he had been in the industry, it always felt good to be recognized for his hard work. But what Mitch said next cooled his happy glow.

"I've also talked to Jasper Kent. He's younger, newer to the scene, but he's a committed rising star. It's too soon to tell. We just don't know yet."

Lincoln snatched the remote from the side table and tried to rewind the segment. He threw the remote when he realized the TV was not equipped to do that. He thought he had heard Mitch announce he was also considering Jasper Kent.

Lincoln grabbed the hotel phone to call his agent. As soon as Dominic answered, Lincoln launched into questions. "Did you know Mitch was considering someone else for this new picture? Am I out here at this godforsaken survival training camp for no damn reason? Because I can hop the next plane and come home right now, if that's the case!"

"Lincoln, baby! I was hoping I'd be on vacation before you heard the news," Dominic chuckled dryly. "Look, nothing is set in stone yet. I spoke with Mitch and, from what he told me, he's considering only the best of the best. You're at the top of the list!"

"That's an LA Maybe, which we both know means bullshit. I'm losing work out here, Dominic."

"No, you're not. You needed the break. You're in overdrive, and what comes after that? Burnout."

"I won't get burnt out," Lincoln grumbled. He rubbed his eyes, feeling tiredness hit him, in contrast to his statement.

"Going to that camp makes you the best actor for the gig. This is great for your image. I already have several reputable entertainment journalists on stand-by who want exclusive interviews when you get back. You'll get the role in Mitch's new film, *and* you'll get big publicity from this."

"I hope you're right. Otherwise, this is all in vain." *Not entirely in vain*, a voice in his head whispered. Lincoln ended the call with his agent and lounged against the pillows at the head of the bed. He was stuck with two very attractive people. He wondered if he would enjoy getting to know them.

Perry was tall, muscular and demanding—a combination that was Lincoln's kryptonite. The minute he had seen the instructor, he had felt a lurch in his core that he knew meant trouble. Likewise, Nadia was a striking woman in every sense of the word. And Lincoln had been so busy lately that sex and titillation had been off-limits. What would happen in the woods with those two?

If for no other reason than to take the break he was being offered, Lincoln needed to stay. He gritted his teeth as he folded his hands behind his head and thought about Jasper Kent being considered for a role that was "perfect" for him.

As rude and untenable as Perry had been thus far, Lincoln could not leave. He had to prove to Mitch Trepan that he was the only person who could play that character. His attraction to his companions be damned.

CHAPTER 2

"Wait, what did you say?" Perry lurched forward in the driver's seat of his truck and pressed the phone closer to his ear.

"Clyde's been hurt!" his neighbor, Mr. Dougal, yelled again. "He fell trying to fix the damned rafters of the barn. The stubborn fool acts like he's pushing thirty not ninety. They think he broke his hip."

"Goddamn it! I told him I would fix the barn! I'm on my way."

"The ambulance come and got him already. We're at the hospital. You might as well meet us here."

The sun was already low in the sky. Perry started the truck and floored the accelerator, glad he had opted to sleep in the parking lot rather than one of the costly hotel rooms.

Clyde MacAskill was all he had left. When his grandparents died, Clyde took him in and raised him as his own. Now that he was getting up in age himself, Perry often worried what he would do when he lost him.

They ran the business together. Perry taught the classes while Clyde handled bookings and manned the radio. It was easier on his rheumatoid arthritis than the work he was doing before. But, if Clyde was hurt, Perry would have to cancel this class.

Could Survive Anything handle another fallow month?

Perry raced the last few blocks to the medical center and rushed into the building. He was greeted by a familiar face at the front desk, a girl he had gone to high school with. "How are you? I'm looking for Clyde MacAskill."

"Doctor's with him. Once he's out, you'll be able to see him." She smiled politely and gestured to the waiting area.

"Thanks," Perry murmured. He made his way to the beat-up plastic chairs where Mr. Dougal sat. Perry shook his hand in appreciation. "How's he doing, Mr. Dougal?"

"None the worse for wear, other than he's mad at himself for slipping. He said you were bringing a class out tomorrow. He don't want you to have to cancel."

"He shouldn't beat himself up. I wouldn't be able to focus on the training course with him hurt, anyway," Perry tried to picture the two bumbling urbanites in the wilderness without Clyde at the cabin to provide a link to civilization. He shivered involuntarily at the nightmarish thought. "Especially not with this set of students," he added.

A nurse stepped through a set of double doors and beckoned Perry. He recognized her, too. Someone else he had gone to school with. "You're here for Mr. McCaskill, right? He's asking for you."

Perry nodded and clasped Mr. Dougal's hand one more time. "Thanks for being a good neighbor, Mr. Dougal. I'll keep you posted."

"Yeah, Sue wants me off the road before it gets dark. Cataracts."

"A wise woman," Perry chuckled. "Drive safely."

He watched his stoop-shouldered neighbor trudge out of the building. Then, he squared his shoulders and braced himself to deal with his stubborn old best friend. He already knew what Clyde would say about a cancelation: *Don't do it.*

Still, Perry would sooner watch his dreams for Survive Anything go down the toilet than neglect someone he loved.

~

N adia stood at the hotel window and stared at the full moon rising over the mountains in the distance. *Beautiful,* she thought. By tomorrow, she would be somewhere in the dense woodlands covering the mountainside, getting up close and personal with nature. *Hopefully, I'll still see the beauty in it.* But with a guide like Perry Evans, that seemed unlikely.

She started at the knock on her door, and then opened it to see her disgruntled instructor. "I had some trouble finding you," Perry muttered. Her eyes skimmed him from head to toe. She ignored the butterflies in her stomach and the spicy scent of his cologne that wafted up her nostrils. He smelled like pine groves and clean mountain air.

Why was he at her room? Her mind exploded with erotic possibilities in that question—images of the sexy instructor throwing her against the wall in a passionate kiss—but the melodramatic thought was so farfetched that she nearly laughed aloud. Never mind her body tingling with misplaced desire. Nadia bit back a smile. "Can I help you?" she asked.

"I need to see you down at the bar in the next thirty minutes. Is that doable?"

"Um, is something wrong?"

"A change of plans. We'll discuss it at the bar. I'm about to let Lincoln know now."

"Okay. I'll be right down." Nadia closed the door and took a deep breath. "Well, what new fuckery is this?" she whispered to herself.

She took a refreshing shower and changed into a black pencil skirt from the carry-on bag she had smuggled past Perry. She buttoned a ruffled blouse over her voluptuous breasts, and she applied lip gloss and mascara, the only make-up in her purse. Everything else was in the luggage she had sent home.

With a toss of her hair, Nadia checked the time and decided to head downstairs early. She ran into Lincoln as she strolled to the elevators. He had changed into red leather pants and a designer shirt. "You kept a bag, too?" she asked.

He flashed a superstar smile that shot sparks. "Apparently great minds think alike. Looking good, Ms. Marson," he murmured. Lincoln put a hand to the base of her spine as he ushered her into the elevator and pressed the button for the lobby.

Oh, he's one of those, Nadia thought. *The open doors and pull out chairs type.* "So, what do you think this sudden change of plans is about?" She moved away from his warm fingertips, sizing him up from the other side of the elevator.

"Who knows? Maybe he's checking to see if we've decided to leave yet. I was *this* close, but I changed my mind," Lincoln said with a laugh.

"Same here. I have my reasons for staying, as I'm sure you do, too," she replied, not bothering to go any deeper. She did not want to give the impression she was interested, although her eyes roamed his body again.

The elevator dinged and bounced slightly as it settled on the ground floor. "After you," Lincoln murmured. He gestured for her to step out.

Nadia smiled in appreciation and strutted across the lobby to the bar where Perry was waiting for them. She was aware that Lincoln's gaze followed the sway of her hips. "Reporting for duty," she announced.

"Is this a do-over of our meet-and-greet? Because I think we got off on the wrong foot." Lincoln grinned and sat beside her.

Perry held up paperwork, saying, "Actually, I called you here for this. These are cancellation and reimbursement forms."

"What! We're both committed to sticking this out, right, Mr. Easley?" Nadia nodded at Lincoln as Perry eyed them both with an apologetic grimace.

"Unfortunately, it's not up to you. I rely on a friend to help out at base camp while we're in the wilderness, and he suffered a fall earlier today that will prevent him from doing that."

"Is he okay?"

"He will be, but if weather conditions get bad or someone gets injured, we don't have a reliable way to call for help. So, I'm canceling this course. You guys should reschedule."

"This is the only time I have available," said Nadia, "and this is important to me. I paid for a unique travel experience. I've been through a hurricane, so I'm okay with bad weather."

"You paid for a unique travel experience and, I suppose, a concierge that bends to your every whim—"

"That's not exactly what I said," Nadia clarified.

Perry spoke over her, "—But this isn't a vacation. It's serious training. If we proceed under these conditions, you do so at your own risk, and you'll have to sign off on that."

"Well, hand over the proper paperwork," Lincoln said gamely. "Finishing Survive Anything is vital to my career, and like Nadia, this is the only downtime in my schedule. It's now or never."

Perry looked disconcerted by their willingness to forge ahead, despite his warnings. Nadia watched his facial expressions transition from annoyance to resolve, but he tried one last time. "Look, no one knows these woods better than me. Based on your level of readiness, I'm not comfortable taking you into the wilderness alone."

"You can't change our minds on this," Nadia stated matter-of-factly.

Perry sighed and pulled out a different set of forms from his battered satchel. "Then, I'll need you to sign *these*, and you can get back to your rooms." He called for the bartender as he handed them the forms. Nadia already felt a tad bit tipsy, but what could one last hurrah with her sexy new travel companions hurt?

L incoln got that he was not the kick-ass action star he played in movies. He was a geeky drama kid at heart and he was fully aware that he was biting off way more than he could chew. Perry's warning rang clear in his ears. But, if Nadia was willing to face the risks, Lincoln had to be bold enough to do so, too. "Another round of drinks!" he shouted gaily, ignoring his own uneasiness.

"Sign the documents first," Perry chuckled, "while you're still clearheaded."

He handed Lincoln a pen, and their hands touched. Lincoln felt warmth spread over his face, but he pretended not to notice the brief skin contact. A holdover from growing up in a small town. *Old habits die hard*, he thought ruefully. As attracted as he was to the domineering military vet, he could not acknowledge the obvious chemistry.

Lincoln maintained a reputation as an All-American manly man, even along the liberal west coast. He ate fast food in public. He drank beers—not the artisanal shit but real American beer with real American names. His style was eye-catching but never androgynous, and his sexuality was never in question.

He had never acted on his urges.

Thoughts and fantasies were easy to ignore when he was busy with work, but this downtime his agent was encouraging him to take with Perry and Nadia opened a Pandora's box of desires he was trying his best to ignore. Adding to the dilemma, Nadia was exactly the type of woman Lincoln liked to have draped on his arm. She was classy, attractive and intelligent. What was not to like?

He signed the paperwork with a flourish, agreeing to this three-week torture, and handed the pen off to Nadia. Within minutes, the deed was done. The dark-haired stunner in the pencil skirt smiled seductively as she slid her drink closer. He watched her pink lips wrap around the straw, and his core tightened with arousal.

"So, since we're stuck with each other," she said, "at least for the next few weeks, I think we should get to know one another. Tell me about yourselves."

"You first," Lincoln suggested. They probably already knew the carefully parsed out personal details handled by his PR team, like where he attended college and how he broke into acting. Very few people knew he had grown up an ostracized, shy young man in a Midwestern town where homogeneity was celebrated and differences were feared and despised.

Nadia took another slow sip which drew his attention to her

delectable mouth. With a toss of her hair, she pinned him with her almond-shaped, chocolate eyes, making Lincoln wonder if she was flirting with him. He could never tell. Again, he felt like his old high school self and not a successful actor.

"What do you want to know?"

"Where you from? What do you do?" he prompted with a shrug.

"Born and raised in Texas, studied at Harvard, doctorate in chemical engineering. There's not much else to me."

"She's being modest. You think you're something, Hollywood?" Perry murmured. Lincoln looked at him in askance. "Ever heard of Marson Oil and Gas? Meet the heiress, Ms. Nadia Marson. You're sitting beside a bona-fide billionaire."

Lincoln's eyebrows shot up in surprise. "Well, this sounds interesting! How does a billionaire end up in a place like this with guys like us? Why sign up for a survival training course when you can just buy your way out of danger?"

"As I told you," Nadia said coolly, "I had first-hand experience with a hurricane. Unfortunately, Death can't be bribed. So, if there's something I can learn that will increase my odds of getting out of a dangerous situation alive, then I'll pay to learn it. And thank you, Perry, for bringing to light something you had no business mentioning."

"Survival requires trust, Ms. Marson. If you need Mr. Evans, here, to ward off the bears while you take a bathroom break, imagine how much more attentive he'll be to the job, knowing your father has money." Perry wore a cheeky half-smile as he swirled his drink around.

"I'm kind of a big deal, too," Lincoln joked. "Just...on a much smaller scale." He beckoned for a refill. The alcohol was already loosening his inhibitions, which was probably a good thing. It was not every day he sat next to a billionaire and a decorated military vet. They were effectively making him feel like the lesser being at the table and the only one with something to prove.

"And, what do you do, Lincoln?" Nadia asked.

He blinked in surprise that she did not already know. "You're pulling my leg. You've never heard of *Vengeance with a Vengeance? Well-worn Suicide Note?*" She shook her head, her expression drawing a blank. "Wow! Watch out for my deflated ego as it whizzes by." He whistled like a balloon losing air as she pulled a face and laughed apologetically.

"Well, I'm sorry! I don't watch many movies. I have a love-hate relationship with celebrity culture."

"Lincoln Easley is our generation's Tom Cruise, minus the creepy Scientology stuff," Perry teased Lincoln, who just rolled his eyes. "High-impact action movies. Lots of explosions, running aimlessly and posing with gun. Minimal dialogue."

"Oh! I knew you looked familiar!" Nadia gushed.

"Liar," Lincoln grumbled.

She giggled. "Okay, you got me, but I'll be sure to check out your work when I get the chance. Is that why you're here?"

"As a matter of fact, it is. I'm preparing for a new role in a man versus nature flick. Once I'm done here, Survive Anything will be a household name."

Perry raised his glass to that. Nadia crossed her legs and turned her attention to him. "And you were a Navy SEAL, a walking lethal weapon. What's that like?" Her voice held a smoky quality that tugged at Lincoln's libido, but she seemed drawn to their instructor. Something they had in common.

"I'm still alive, so I guess it's been good to me." Perry smiled charmingly.

"No fair. You know more about us than we know about you." Nadia pouted at his non-answer.

"Well, unlike you and Hollywood, I don't need money or fame as an incentive for you to cover my ass if a bear attacks. I'll be the only one out there with the tools and skills necessary to keep you alive, and that's all you need to know."

"Point taken." Lincoln chuckled as he tossed back another shot and thumped the glass on the countertop with a gasp at the fiery liquor burning down his chest. "Why did you get out of the military?"

Perry's playful smile slipped away. "Injury," he muttered laconically. He gestured at his shoulder. Lincoln took in his muscular upper body with envy and appreciation. Perry radiated strength and capability, not like someone who would be slowed down by a bum shoulder.

"Couldn't you have transitioned to something else military-related?"

"I'm not a desk-job kinda guy," Perry grunted.

It was clear he had no desire to talk about it, and Lincoln let the subject drop. An awkward silence descended as he glanced from Perry to Nadia. *Eye candy all around*, he thought.

"So…" She drew the word out, flashing a tiny smile because he was staring.

Perry looked at the time and gathered his satchel. "So, it's getting late. You guys need your rest. We'll be leaving at eight in the morning, and everything from here on out will be strenuous. Sleep tight."

"Wait a minute." Lincoln halted him with a hand on his shoulder. He quickly removed his hand when that zing of electric desire came back. The word 'strenuous' only intensified it. He could think of a few strenuous activities he wanted to engage in with the man rising from the barstool. "Don't you want one more round before we go?"

"I think we've had enough for one night," Perry declined.

Lincoln snorted in amusement. "C'mon! In a few days, we'll hate your guts. We're close to that now, as a matter of fact. Tonight, let's enjoy each other. Have a couple drinks! Sing off-key!"

"Sing off-key? Now, you're pushing it," Perry chuckled. He rubbed the back of his neck and looked around self-consciously when Lincoln insistently nudged him back to his barstool. "Alright, alright! One more drink."

Nadia leaned toward him. "Lincoln's right, you know. You probably have a certain way you handle your students, but I like to think he and I aren't the usual. You can come out of your cocoon with us."

"No, you're not my usual. But, what makes you think I'm in a cocoon?"

"Well, for one thing, you look very uptight right now—stiff shoulders, arms crossed, blank face."

"This is my relaxed look," Perry scoffed.

Lincoln and Nadia shared a laugh. "Yeah, he's loosening up, but I think he definitely needs another drink." Nadia clapped her hands and summoned the bartender. "What are you having, Perry? I insist, one last round on me."

"I'll have a seltzer then."

Nadia clasped Lincoln's forearm in feigned dismay. "Did he say seltzer? Oh, no! Somebody, get this man a gin and tonic, pronto!"

CHAPTER 3

Perry shook his head in amazement, hardly believing he was letting down his guard with these two. The bartender brought him a gin and tonic, he took a tentative sip and let the conversation flow around him. Five minutes into the easy banter, his glass was empty.

He ordered another drink, knowing he was breaking protocol. *Gotta keep the clients happy*, he told himself. Even his hotel choice reflected the fact Nadia Marson and Lincoln Easley were rich and famous. An endorsement from either of them would go a long way to helping his business.

Clyde was resting comfortably at the hospital and had plans to spend a few weeks with his great-granddaughter upon release. Perry wanted to be on stand-by if his old friend needed him, but Clyde had made it clear he expected him to work.

Perry fired off a text to let him know Survive Anything would keep its prestigious new students. When Clyde responded with a thumbs-up and smiley face emoticons, he chuckled and put his phone away. *One less thing to worry about*. He could focus on Lincoln and Nadia.

The actor had been preening since hearing Nadia was a billionaire, but the liquor was having the intended effect. Lincoln gradually became less self-conscious and stopped grand-standing, and they chatted about their interests while Perry listened.

He liked how Nadia gave her full attention. He studied the way her hair draped her shoulders. The light fell on her high cheekbones and made her eyes deep and mysterious. Her mouth was expressive, even when she was not speaking—lips turning up in a smile when amused, parting slightly when surprised.

She was adept at making a person feel special, despite her obvious wealth. *Very down-to-earth*, Perry thought. She was also spoiled of course, and it showed in subtle ways—like when the bartender let her glass get empty, and Nadia shot him a look that guaranteed he would never repeat the error.

Perry studied Lincoln, with his perfect wavy hair falling over his handsome face. Was Nadia interested in the debonair thespian? He tried to find something not to like about him. For one thing, Lincoln was full of himself. They were bound to bump heads at some point.

He was dressed too stylishly for drinks at a bar but Perry did like Lincoln's choice of bold colors. His wardrobe emphasized a gym-honed physique that said he put a lot of effort into his appearance. Was that a strike against him or not? Perry could not decide.

Lincoln noticed him staring and laughed nervously. "What is it? Do I have something in my teeth?"

"Not at all. Your smile is perfect."

"That's nice of you to say to him! Wait, how many drinks have you had?" Nadia arched a brow.

"Apparently enough," Perry allowed. "More than the 'one more round' you requested. Now, it's almost nine o'clock. If we don't retire, we'll all regret it come sunrise."

Nadia's pink tongue swept the bow of her lips, and Perry stared at her mouth, aching. He balled a fist to resist the temptation to touch her. Finally, she nodded in agreement. "I guess that means the party's over."

"Can I see you to your room?" Lincoln piped up.

Perry was caught off guard by the suggestion, especially when he realized Lincoln was talking to *him*. "Um, I'm not staying in the hotel."

Lincoln: "Where are you staying?"

"In my truck in the parking lot."

Nadia's jaw dropped. "Perry, that has to be god-awful uncomfortable. I get that you're channeling the capable survival instructor, but who's going to regret *that* come sunrise? You can't sleep in a truck."

"Look, don't worry about me. I do it all the time. Go get some rest. Goodnight Ms. Marson, Mr. Easley." Perry grabbed his satchel and turned away before getting dragged into a debate about where he would sleep, but Lincoln stopped him in his tracks with his next statement.

"Why don't you share my room?" he blurted out.

"I don't think that will be…" Perry met his gaze. He was about to say 'necessary,' but something else tumbled from his lips. "…wise."

Nadia interrupted the intense eye contact. "I upgraded to the presidential suite."

"Yeah, I noticed that when I came to get you for the meeting. So much for the austere living of a naturist," Perry said with a wry smile.

"Hey, don't judge me. A girl's gotta have her hot tub. Anyway, there's plenty of space, and you can sleep in the sitting room so you can have some privacy. What do you say?"

"Am I the only one without a hot tub?"

"You can come, too, Lincoln!" Nadia offered.

Against his better judgement, Perry found himself following them to the elevator bay. He was pleasantly buzzed from the gin and tonic, but not soused enough to not hear the voice of reason telling him to pivot and head to the parking lot. He knew what he was supposed to do, but the rules seemed to have changed. Also, he really did need that good review.

The chummy night would likely set the tone for the rest of their stay, but Perry needed to keep some boundaries in place. He was the teacher and they were the students, albeit two of the sexiest students he had ever met. Both turned him on in ways he could not explain. They both seemed to know how to make him abandon reason. He never had drinks with his students. Lines had already been crossed.

And it was too late to go back now. Perry stepped into the elevator and the doors whispered shut. Nadia smiled coyly. "Is there a Mrs. Evans at home who might be offended by you spending the night in my room?" she asked.

"I'm not in a relationship. Eighth floor, right?"

Lincoln murmured, "Yeah. My room is right down from hers. Can't believe I don't have a hot tub."

Nadia bubbled with laughter. "Stop pouting. I told you that you can come hang out in mine. What about you, Hollywood? Are you dating anybody?"

"Why? Interested?" Lincoln gave her a slow once over.

"Asking for a friend," she chuckled.

Perry replied matter of factly, "Hey, here's a friendly reminder: No fraternizing on my watch. We'll have enough to worry about when we get in the woods. The last thing I need is two love birds trying to turn this into a hook-up session."

"We're not in the woods yet," Lincoln stated. Nadia eased between Perry and the panel of numbers. "Besides, I don't think I'm the one you have to worry about."

"Don't be melodramatic, Lincoln. I was just going to ask Perry if he does this with all his students."

"Of course, not," Perry sighed. He shook his head and stepped away from her.

"Then, we should feel special?" she asked in jest.

"I think it's my turn to ask *you* how much you've had to drink."

"Enough, apparently."

Her sensual kiss came out of nowhere. Her full breasts collided with his chest, and her soft lips molded to his. *How much was enough?* Perry wondered. *Too much?*

"Ms. Marson...You don't know what you're getting into," he exhaled as she drove him to the wall and continued the lingering kiss. His body hardened, even as he tried to pump the brakes.

"Jeez! Get a room," Lincoln chuckled.

The elevator dinged on her floor. Nadia walked out with a sway of her hips, steady on her feet and clear-eyed. Perry realized she was not drunk; she was in full control of herself. "I have a room," she tossed over her shoulder. She looked back at them and smiled seductively. "Are you two coming or not?"

~

A s soon as the door to her hotel suite slammed shut, Perry pulled her into his arms and continued what she had instigated in the elevator. His hands raced over her body. His lips collided with hers in a bruising kiss, and his tongue speared deep, but the rough-handling spiked her lust.

She cast a wild glance over her shoulder as Perry kissed down her neck. She saw Lincoln leaning against the door, staring unabashedly. *She had invited them both.* The thought kept repeating itself. *She had invited them both.* What was she doing?

Perry's open-mouthed kisses swept like liquid fire over her skin and clouded her senses. Her heart raced in her heaving chest, and her pulse quickened. Sensibility was supposed to kick in at any second. Only it never got the memo. He raked his hands down the front of her blouse and tore it open. She heard buttons rain to the floor. He stared at her exposed skin with wide open eyes tinted with rampant arousal.

He took a step back, and his broad shoulders rose and fell as he sucked in a deep breath; he was fighting for self-control. He swiped a hand over his beautiful mouth, and all she could think was, *Damn, I want his mouth on me.* The ridge of his erection strained his jeans. She shifted her weight from one foot to the other under his intense scrutiny, but that just served to make her clit throb even more.

"You should tell me to stop," he warned.

"No." She lifted her head defiantly. "I don't want to stop."

He nodded as if he knew she would say as much. As he gave her another slow perusal, she stared at his crotch, decadent thoughts swirling in her head. "Are you sure this is what you want?" he asked. Her eyes snapped back to his.

She gathered the bottom of his black t-shirt and dragged him flush against her aching body. "This is what I want," she whispered.

His burning mouth nuzzled past the black lace of her bra. Sparks showered in the dark when he found her nipple. She clasped the back of his neck and pressed him to her chest. *Yes!* The ghost of the word flowed from her lips. She stared at the ceiling, eyelids fluttering in ecstasy. *Oh, God, yes!*

His thigh slipped between her legs and grinded against her throbbing pussy. His rigid cock nudged her lower stomach. She thought she would pop from excitement. She reached down to touch him. His erection hard and heavy against her palm made it all very real.

She was in a strange town with two strange men. Her dad would have a fit if he knew. But this was one time the wealthy heiress wanted to rebel, and it did not matter what Wilson Marson thought as he would never know.

Perry boldly cupped her saturated womanhood. She hissed his name when he stroked her through the thin fabric of her panties. Over his shoulder, she saw Lincoln's reflection in a mirror mounted on the wall. He was masturbating. His hand gently squeezed and released a thick cord bulging the front of his slacks. For some reason, that turned her on even more.

Groaning, she canted her pelvis forward, deeper into Perry's hand. His fingers slipped past her underwear, and he touched her slick, dewy labia. He probed deeper. She hitched in a breath when he pushed a digit inside of her. In and out, he stroked, making her hotter and wetter. Tantalizing her.

She bit her bottom lip and hummed in anticipation as he walked her backward to the door. Suddenly, she slammed into Lincoln's muscular chest and let out a surprised gasp. She was sandwiched between the two men with Lincoln's pulsating erection against her lush derriere and Perry's thick cock against her front.

"Mm!" Lincoln groaned. He was tense and stiff, hardly breathing as his fingertips lightly skimmed her stomach. She felt him trembling with self-restraint.

Perry stared her in the eyes and asked again: "What about this? Is *this* what you want?" She knew what he was asking. *Did she want to have a threesome?* Her answer should have been no, but...

Nadia contemplated what would happen if she said yes.

Lincoln's hands moved up her torso. She did not stop him. He cupped her breasts and kneaded the sensitive peaks. Her nipples turned to shards of glass beneath his touch. At the same time, his moist lips trailed hot kisses along the side of her neck.

And she almost said it.

Perry peeled off her shirt and released her bra, sucking her breasts with powerful drags of his mouth. He brought her leg over his hip and grinded against her. She countered his thrusts.

The word was on the tip of her tongue.

Lincoln bunched up her pencil skirt. She felt him fumbling with his pants, heard the zipper release. His hot, hard cock emerged. Then, he eased his lower body forward, and she felt him against her bare ass where her G-string disappeared. She quaked with arousal and nervousness, but she let them do it.

She wanted to blame her behavior on having had too much to drink, although she knew that was not the case. Maybe it was her self-imposed half-year of celibacy. Maybe it was the company she was keeping. Together, they were twice as irresistible.

"Yes!" she breathed.

Perry stopped, as if to make sure he had heard her correctly. "Yes?" he asked.

She strutted to the mattress and dropped to the cool duvet. She unzipped her skirt and tossed it away and was now wearing nothing but her red-bottom heels and the G-string.

CHAPTER 4

He wanted them both. Perry tried to ignore his reaction to the insanely attractive man. It was Nadia who had invited them to indulge her wildest fantasies. This was about her. He was shocked by the turn of events that had placed him in the billionaire's bedroom, but there was no stopping this train now.

Perry unwrapped a condom and fell between Nadia's legs. He slipped inside with a quiet grunt of pleasure, and her eyes widened in ecstasy. Lincoln studied the way he clasped her hips and rocked in and out, and he touched himself with growing excitement.

Perry's muscular body gleamed in the moonlight, abs clenching and releasing as he had his way with her. Intense rapture gave him a look of concentration. Her unblemished skin glowed. Her flat stomach quivered, and she tried to hold in her sobs of bliss, but Perry's increasingly forceful thrusts pressed the moans from her.

Watching Perry sexily bite his bottom lip made lust shoot through Lincoln like an arrow. This was not sex; it was some other magic. Something that kneaded and pounded his psyche until his body—dangling over the precipice of completion—threatened to let go.

He climbed in bed and collected Nadia's lush breasts in hand.

Moaning, he dropped butterfly kisses over her lips, but he could not keep his eyes off Perry, who was busy gliding in and out of her pussy.

Nadia brushed a hand down Lincoln's torso toward his engorged manhood. She masturbated him slowly and deliberately—the same way Perry was taking care of her body—drawing forth pre-cum and making Lincoln gasp her name.

"Lincoln is getting left out," she whispered.

"Are you ready for him?" Perry asked.

"He's all yours," she said.

Lincoln froze in shock as she took Perry's hand and brought it to his manhood. "Wait—what are we doing?" he asked breathlessly.

Nadia managed a half-shrug. "Experimenting?"

All three of them stared at Lincoln's massive erection. At the way Perry's hand made his hips yo-yo up and down involuntarily. Lincoln thrusted into his palm, grunting in pleasure when he stroked the head of his cock.

To him, Perry seemed intent on doing whatever Nadia desired. If she got her kicks from pairing them together, then Perry seemed on board. But what did that mean? Lincoln was not sure why she had initiated this, and his heightened arousal made it difficult to parse out her motivations. He did not want to think, he just wanted to feel.

Nadia kissed the side of his neck as Perry jerked him off. "No one has to know," she whispered in Lincoln's ear. He passionately kissed her to silence her nonsense. It was not about anyone else knowing. *They* would know.

Lincoln clenched his eyes shut. He was close to coming from what Perry was doing to him, but he cried out in sheer astonishment when someone's plush lips wrapped around his cock. Was it Nadia or Perry? He refused to look. He allowed himself to be taken deeper into the unknown.

Silky wetness enveloped his erection, and whatever reserve he had maintained disappeared. He reemerged slowly and plunged in again. Tremulous moans escaped him as he kept going, and his skin tingled with anticipation as he drilled in and out of Nadia's perfect mouth.

He knew it was her by the way she hummed and sent vibrations running through his cock. At the same time, Perry's hand swept up and down his shaft, chasing the trail her mouth left. A spasm shot through Lincoln's testes. The pressure built.

"Huh!" he gasped, pulling away.

Nadia whimpered, and Lincoln heard the unmistakable sound of the other two kissing. He felt lightheaded, unable to move. Any shift would create an eruption. So, he sat still and listened to their growing enthrallment.

"We shouldn't be doing this," Perry moaned, kissing her harder.

"Do you want to stop?" Nadia panted.

"Damn it, Nadia! Don't ask me that," he said.

"Answer the question!"

"No!" Perry growled.

He cradled her head and guided her mouth back to Lincoln's erection. Lincoln sucked in a breath as her soft lips enveloped him, and her velvety tongue swirled around the sensitive tip. She devoured him like she had waited a lifetime to taste him, like she was begging for him to blast off. Her eager mouth swallowed him whole in an oasis of heat and wetness that made Lincoln shudder.

Her head bobbed faster up and down at his pelvis. Lincoln clutched a fistful of her hair and held her in place for deep strokes of his throbbing cock. He gasped as his thighs bunched. His abs clenched. He almost—Almost! "Oh, my God! Where do you want it?" Lincoln all but begged to come. With a broken moan, he let her go, and she looked up at him with a seductive smile.

"Kinky," she whispered. "But not yet…"

Lincoln shook his head deliriously. "I can't hold out."

"Yes, you can." She turned her face to Perry, who sat on his knees beside them. Her red lips swept over the other man's erection, and Perry surged into her mouth with an agonized cry of passion. For some reason, it turned Lincoln on even more. He tangled his fingers in her hair and guided her to do to Perry what she had done to him.

But she needed no help. She expertly sucked him off. Lincoln tried not to stare as her mouth danced up and down, flashing X-rated glimpses. Instead, he focused on Nadia's sexy hourglass figure, her heart-shaped ass beckoning in the dark. Never mind that his gaze kept straying to Perry's impressive erection, rippling with veins, the head a tantalizing deep purple. He licked his lips.

"You don't have to resist it," Perry murmured.

"What?" Lincoln looked up and realized the instructor was staring at him intently.

"You can do what you want. We've already gone too far. I'm not gonna stop you."

"What do you think I...?"

Perry grabbed him by the neck and closed the distance between them. His lips met Lincoln's in a soul-stirring kiss. It was like being struck by lightning. *Electric.* Invisible sparks showered around them. When Perry wove his tongue through his mouth, Lincoln swallowed his raspy moans. The kiss seemed to last an eternity.

Lincoln melted in his arms, letting Perry ease him to the bed and work a condom over his pulsating dick. He could not recall ever wanting anyone else as much. He hardly noticed Nadia straddling him. Not until she took him inside of her saturated sheath. He pulled away from Perry to look at where the sensual goddess ensnared him.

As she lowered herself to bury him to the hilt, Lincoln exhaled shakily, and his eyes rolled back. But he also reached blindly for Perry. Nadia moaned and rocked with a delicious sway of her hips, and Lincoln found Perry's erection. The buff survival instructor rose on his knees at Lincoln's head. Without thinking, Lincoln hungrily swallowed him.

Perry gripped a fistful of his hair and rammed deeper. His primal growl filled the room, and Lincoln tasted the tart, tangy flavor of his pre-cum. Lincoln kissed his way down Perry's thick shaft. His tongue darted into the slit at the head of his cock. Perry sobbed his name. Lincoln fired a thin stream of spit and worked it around with his hand.

The oral sex was messy and ungraceful, but he did not care. It was what he wanted. Nadia's pussy squeezed him a tight paradise, and Perry surged in and out of his mouth. Groaning, Lincoln gripped Nadia's hips and thrust up and into her harder, feeling her thighs clench around him. Perry quaked on his tongue. This would be over all too soon.

"Yes," Perry gasped. "Ah, fuck, yes!"

Just this once Lincoln felt he could be himself. *A little longer*, he pleaded inwardly. He wanted to be free a little longer.

~

Perry clutched the base of his cock, diving in and out of Lincoln's soaking wet mouth. His testosterone peaked. He had been inside of Nadia's lush body, and that had been exquisite. But this...this was his forbidden fantasy. It obliterated lonely nights of 'What If' questions about his sexuality.

He could not believe he was letting it happen, and he could not believe he had waited so late in life to do what he desired. Lincoln greedily sucked his dick as Perry caressed his face, fondling the bold curve of his jawline. He forced himself to watch the act taking place. To see a man's mouth around his cock. To experience the electrifying wonder of it.

"Have you done this before?" Perry asked breathlessly. Lincoln hummed dissent. This was new for him, too, and he seemed to be enjoying it. "That's it...Just like that. Uhn! Yes!"

Nadia whined as the sex intensified. Her body jostled in Lincoln's arms, drawing Perry's attention. He drank in the sight of her. The rise and fall made her breasts jiggle invitingly. She stroked her clit in swift circles, riding Lincoln with expert finesse, a carousel of seduction. Perry watched the place where she connected with Lincoln and saw her creamy nectar spill down his thick cock.

The erotic sight made him push deeper into Lincoln's mouth. With every moan of Lincoln's pleasure, Perry felt the reverberations through his erection. Nadia raked her fingers through Perry's hair and dragged him to her lips. "Is it good?" she whispered, kissing him. Perry moaned, unable to speak. He could hardly think.

He felt brittle, breakable, as if he would shatter the instant he reached the pinnacle. Lincoln gasped and sucked him with abandon. He wrapped his arms around Nadia to hammer harder. Perry stared in awe at the way they grinded together. He could almost taste the tension in the room. Suddenly, she added her tongue to the melee, vying with Lincoln to suck him off.

And Perry knew he was through. "I'm gonna come!" he groaned. Her silky hair flowed through his fingers as he cupped the back of her head and fed her his erection. Lincoln sucked and nibbled his balls. Nadia's velvety tongue laved his cock as Perry bit back a sob of elation. His abs tensed when Nadia pressed his shaft between both her and Lincoln's mouths, and they kissed around his pounding hard-on.

The slick, decadent sound of fiercely escalating sex accompanied Perry's rapid ascent to heaven. He shook his head in denial, and tried to count, in an attempt to distract himself, but it did not work. He was about to blow. He growled through clenched teeth and rushed in and out of the gap between Nadia and Lincoln's lips. Unexpectedly, Lincoln took him balls deep, and that was the final straw. Perry flinched.

Pleasure tore through him. He gripped Lincoln's wavy hair. Growling, he drilled deeper and faster with the spirals of ecstasy rippling swiftly outward from his pelvis. At the same time, Nadia erupted with soprano wails as she raced to the finish line.

Her orgasm was a beautiful sight. Her lustrous hair floated around her thrashing face as she threw her head back, screaming in bliss. Lincoln groaned deep in his throat as her release rippled around his cock, and Perry felt the reverberations through every inch of his being.

He tried not to cry out, but the rapture was too great. He exploded in Lincoln's mouth with a loud howl of completion that joined Nadia's whimpers. A rush of hot jizz shot over Lincoln's lips and tongue. Perry stared in awe. He should have been turned off, but the image seared into his brain, unforgettable.

"What are you doing to me? What are you doing?" Perry stammered. Lincoln licked and sucked the silky white elixir with no qualms, cleaning his quivering cock until Perry clasped his face and kissed him. He channeled his excitement with the slant of his mouth and stroke of his tongue. He tasted himself. Lincoln tasted like him.

As Perry fell to the bed, spent, Lincoln rolled Nadia onto her back and dragged her legs over his hips. She locked her feet at the ankles behind him. He hammered her receptive body and chased the lightning the two of them had already ridden. Perry stared at his handsome face, contorted in a determined scowl. His open mouth begged for more kisses. Perry boldly moved closer to give him more.

As soon as their lips met again, Lincoln whimpered and came undone. He said Perry's name in a way that made the hardened military vet shake uncontrollably. Lincoln clung desperately to him as he orgasmed inside of Nadia's perfect embrace.

When it was done, Perry dragged him into his arms, tore off the condom and touched Lincoln's sputtering erection. The last drops of his spunk drizzled on Perry's fingertips, and he tentatively brought the droplets to his tongue. Lincoln shuddered, watching him.

Gradually, in the dark, quiet room, the madness passed. Lincoln pulled away. The three of them lay in Nadia's hotel bed, breathing heavily and recovering from what had happened. Perry's pounding heart slowed to normal rate, and he heaved a sigh, taking stock.

What in God's name had he let happen? He was slightly ashamed at losing control with his students but mostly confused about why any of it had happened. He also wondered how he was supposed to take them into the woods after this.

"I'm sorry. This shouldn't have...It never happened, alright?" he murmured.

Lincoln instantly nodded in agreement, but Nadia sat up on her elbow and looked at each of them. "So, we pretend the chemistry between us isn't off the charts? I mean, we *can*," she said pointedly, "but I think it'll be difficult to play it off...once we get in the woods where we can do more things that 'no one has to know.'"

Lincoln abruptly reached for his clothes. "Perry's right. Let's pretend like this never happened. It was a one-night stand. One-night stands don't count, long as we never mention this again."

"Two against one. You both hated it. Got it." She arched a manicured brow skeptically. Lincoln refused to meet her gaze.

Perry swung his legs to the side of the bed and rose to his feet. "I'm taking a shower and returning to my truck," he announced. He could kick himself for coming up to her room. *Big mistake.* He brushed past Lincoln who was already half-dressed, and the actor averted his gaze from his nakedness.

"I can't believe we did this," Lincoln mumbled. "This isn't how I was raised. *Normal* men and women don't hook up like this—not even in the loose and easy twenty-first century. It's...It's unnatural."

Perry suppressed a snort. "No, it's not."

"It's human nature," said Nadia. "Okay, we had a threesome! People do it all the time. We tried it out; you guys didn't like it; so, we move on with our lives. But, Perry, I'm not letting you sleep in that truck. Stay in the sitting room, like we agreed."

Perry quietly slipped into the *en suite* and powered on the showerhead without responding to her. He understood threesomes, even if in the past, his experiences excluded same-sex intercourse. What he did not understand was how a woman like Nadia could be okay with seeing two men suck each other off and why she seemed to want an encore.

He pictured the next three weeks in the woods and realized the billionaire had a point. It would be impossible to pretend there was no interest once they were alone together. No one there to see. No one there to tell. Just three weeks of alone time with nature. Human nature.

As Perry stepped out of the shower and put on one of the hotel robes, he also considered Lincoln's reaction. The actor clearly had reservations about what had gone down. Yet, in the heat of the moment, Lincoln had been all in. It was not Perry's imagination that he had enjoyed every second of it. So, why suddenly put up a big front?

He exited the bathroom and saw Nadia brushing her hair at the mirror. She seemed completely content. "I meant what I said about staying the night," she reiterated.

He asked, "Do I have a choice?"

She flashed a half-smile as she grabbed her belongings and slipped into the bathroom after him. "Get a blanket and make yourself at home."

Perry felt awkward about it. And when he entered the sitting room and found Lincoln pacing, the sense of awkwardness amplified. "I thought you were leaving," Perry muttered. He pulled a throw off the back of the sofa and plumped a pillow. No point in going to his truck. What was done, was done. Sighing, he made himself comfortable.

Lincoln sat across from him on the loveseat. "Listen, I think we should get a few things straight," he said.

"Pun intended, I presume?"

Lincoln colored. "No, I'm not—I don't want you to think that what happened between us means I'm gay."

"Neither am I." Perry closed his eyes and crossed his arms over his chest. He could feel the nervous energy radiating off his counterpart, but he did not want to deal with it. The event was too raw; he needed to process the whys and wherefores, and he could not do that with Lincoln sitting there.

Perry still wanted him. He wanted a do-over—less spontaneous combustion and more slow burn—so he could figure out if the attraction was mutual or just something Nadia had orchestrated for her own gratification. And, if she had, why? Why had Lincoln gone along with it so enthusiastically? Perry opened his eyes a fraction. "Still there?"

Lincoln moved from the loveseat and kneeled before him. "If you're not...," he trailed off. "I mean, if we're not gonna do this again, I want to know for sure this was a fluke."

Perry shifted to study him.

Lincoln impulsively leaned in and captured his lips in a sultry kiss that made the blood rush in Perry's ears. He clenched the blanket to keep from pulling him closer, a moan rising in his throat. Lincoln's mouth melded with his, and their tongues warred. Their breathing escalated. The fire was back, stronger than ever. Lincoln broke the kiss with a startled gasp. They studied each other in silence. It was not a fluke.

Perry laid a hand on Lincoln's upper thigh. "You might as well shower here and stay the night," he said.

CHAPTER 5

The next morning, Nadia rose from the tangled sheets and crossed the bedroom. She peered out and saw Perry stirring and Lincoln asleep in the sitting room, and she quickly closed the door. *So, it had not been a dream then.*

"What did I do?" she squeaked quietly. *You had a kinky bisexual threesome last night, that's what,* her inner voice chided. Nadia considered herself a modern woman—one who respected a person's right to fully embrace his or her sexuality—but what she had done last night had broken all the rules.

She caught a glimpse of herself in the mirror across from the bed. Her hair fell around her wide-eyed face, bestowing an innocent look she most certainly did not warrant. She grabbed the bedcovers and wrapped them around her naked body, counting down to the explosion of shame she was certain would come.

But it did not come. She was shameless. Literally. She had no shame. Delicious memories came flooding back to her. Having two men at once was like having her cake and eating it, too, and Nadia Marson just loved her cake.

Her six-month streak of celibacy had been a vital part of getting over Jason Stratham. She had not intended to end that run, but last night the fates had conspired to deliver an invitation that she could not refuse.

Now it was time to assess the damage. Lincoln and Perry had gotten to see the real her down at the bar the prior evening. What would they think of her this morning? She was currently the only girl in a class with two alpha males. She wanted to show them she could work as hard and certainly didn't want them treating her with kid gloves.

She realized that it would be crazy to do the course. She didn't fall in love with every man she slept with, but dangerous situations had a way of bonding people. Besides, things were already awkward between them. She hardly wanted to face them, and she doubted being confined together for three weeks would make it any easier.

Nadia shook her head at herself as she dressed. She would have to leave. *Sign the reimbursement forms and book a flight home*, she ordered herself. If she was lucky, her father would give up trying to hire her and let her move on with her life in peace. She stepped into the suite's lounge to announce her decision.

Before she could speak, Perry gruffly pointed at the breakfast spread on the table by the window. "Bulk up. You'll need the protein."

So much for pleasantries, she thought. Nadia smiled weakly and obediently put food on a saucer, but her stomach churned as she surveyed the room. There was no way she could eat. Perry sat on the loveseat, and Lincoln lounged against the wall. No eye contact and very limited small talk. The entire scene cemented her resolve to cut her losses and sign up for a survival course under someone else.

"Guys, I can't do this." She dumped her saucer as Lincoln raised a brow.

Perry stopped eating. "Can't do what?" he asked.

Her hotel phone rang. *Saved by the bell.* She quickly excused herself to avoid explaining her out-of-the-blue surrender. How could she get out of this trip without looking like she was running scared? She answered the phone, hoping it was Maria, her assistant, her pedicurist—hell, anyone who could give her a reason to jet. Anyone *except* Wilson Marson.

"This is Nadia speaking."

"Oh, good! You haven't left the hotel yet!" Her father's boomed and Nadia cringed. "Where did you say you lost your cellphone? I've been trying to call you since last night. Your assistant reminded me to try the hotel."

"Uh, we gave our cellphones to the instructor when we got here. It's part of the training. No technology and all that. Is everything okay?" *Tell me the dog is sick. Give me an excuse to come home that doesn't involve that stupid job.*

"No, everything is not okay. Last night, the board of directors was compelled to remove an upper level researcher from the lab, and the vacancy needs to be filled quickly; I told them you would be the perfect candidate."

Nadia covered her face and shook her head. "Dad, please don't tell me you had someone fired just to get me to work for you," she groaned.

"Of course, not," Wilson said indignantly. "As it turns out, Dr. Calicut is under investigation for plagiarism. This comes at the worst possible time. The optics are terrible. But if I can get you in place soon enough, maybe we can keep things running smoothly. I have a small team ready to bring you up to speed on your job duties. How soon can you fly out?"

"Dad, I didn't want to get into this with you again, but you know I think we have an ethical responsibility to—"

"Yes, we've been over it a thousand times," he interjected, "and you know we go above and beyond our ethical responsibility to provide clean energy without sacrificing the livelihoods of millions of people. We even go the extra mile by funding research on our impact on the environment."

"And research has shown that we are *drastically* impacting the environment," Nadia fumed.

"C'mon, honey. Gimme a break! Research also shows that we're past the tipping point as far as the environment goes. The damage was done by others before us, and you needn't feel guilty for taking your place in the Marson Oil and Gas empire. Besides, if you want to change the world, you have to work from the inside."

Nadia squeezed her eyes shut. As much as she wanted to run away from her entanglement with Perry and Lincoln, she wanted to run away from her "place in the Marson Oil and Gas empire" even more. She had no idea she was crying angry tears until Perry touched her face. She nearly jumped off the bed.

"I didn't mean to scare you. Is everything okay? Sounds like a heated conversation," he whispered.

Nadia dashed her tears. "No, yeah, sorry. Important call. I'll be right out after this." He hesitated, studying her closely, but she forced a smile. "Seriously, I'm fine."

"Does it have anything to do with you saying you can't do this?" Perry gestured back and forth between them. She bit her bottom lip, wanting to tell him yes—Wilson Marson had everything to do with why she could not get involved with him and Lincoln—but her father's summons was not the escape route she wanted.

"No, I was, um, talking about breakfast. I couldn't eat. But I'm definitely still on for the trip."

Her father cut in, "Who are you talking to, Nadia?"

"Just the...staff." She gestured for Perry to leave. His expression darkened at her choice of words, but he exited without comment. Returning to the phone call, Nadia let out a slow breath. "Alright, I'll take the position."

"Thank you." The sincerity in her father's voice touched her, but it also reminded her of the complications ahead. She wanted to make her father proud, but she wanted to be able to live with herself.

Her father was not the heartless one-percenter fueled by greed that his critics believed him to be. He had inherited his role at the helm of the family empire the same way she would eventually inherit hers. That said, the legacy they left behind for future Clarks and the rest of humanity mattered.

Her father teasingly called her a product of her Ivy League education. She was more than that; nothing was ever that simple. Growing up as the daughter of an oil magnate, Nadia knew climate change was bad, but energy was necessary. She also knew she could not avoid her responsibilities forever.

A Marson always rises to the occasion, she thought glumly. She could only stall, and stall she would. "I'll accept the position on one condition," she amended. "Let me finish this survival course with Lincoln and Perry. Give me three weeks in nature to clear my head."

"Lincoln and Perry?"

"My classmate and my instructor." Nadia blushed.

"I'm not sure I like the idea of you being in the woods with two strange men. You didn't mention that yesterday when we spoke."

She rolled her eyes. "Dad, they're completely harmless, and I'm twenty—"

"I know. You're not my little girl anymore; you're a grown woman. You can have your three weeks, but be good out there. Sometimes it's not what you do. It's how it looks. After that nasty situation with Jason Stratham, I don't want you in the tabloids again."

"Of course. I'll keep that in mind," she said. He was right. There was no telling who might be watching and waiting to tear down her good name. This situation would be trickier than she thought.

Lincoln breezed through the lobby in Nadia and Perry's wake. His neck ached from sleeping on the loveseat, but he ignored it. He did not know why he had accepted Perry's offer to spend the night, retiring to their separate places and pretending like nothing stirred in the darkness between them. But he had gotten the answer to his inner questions. The kiss said it all.

The kiss made Lincoln want to break away from the trio and get a cab to the nearest airport. The only thing keeping him from leaving was the fact Nadia was not running away. Both Nadia and Perry seemed to have no trouble keeping up appearances. For a seasoned actor like Lincoln, it should not have been difficult, but it was.

His eyes strayed to the flyaway curls at the nape of Nadia's neck. Her hair was pulled up in a ponytail that showed off her angular cheekbones. He studied the snug fit of Perry's jeans and the way his black t-shirt hugged his muscular torso. Lincoln closed his eyes to keep from staring, but flashbacks of the previous evenings events held him hostage.

Perry stopped walking when they encountered a crowd of people waiting to check out. Lincoln sensed a shift in his mood, from brooding to downright moody. Perry narrowed his eyes and beckoned for Nadia and Lincoln to hang back. "We'll let them get out of the way, first," he muttered.

Nodding, Lincoln absently swiped a brochure from a display table nearby. On the front of the glossy piece of paper was a photograph of a burly man wearing supple leather and a dream catcher necklace. The print advertised, "Come discover the secrets to Empowered Survival!" Inside the brochure were images of people swimming tranquilly in hot springs, rock climbing, sitting around campfires.

Lincoln was surprised to see the man on the front of the brochure standing with the group at the front desk. "You know that guy?" He flashed the pamphlet at Perry.

"Yep. Rick Feldman."

"The competition?"

Perry merely nodded. Lincoln knew a thing or two about competition. Lincoln wished that his own competition, Jasper Kent, would take a hike. *But I'm the one headed for a walk in the woods.*

The broad-shouldered man in fatigues from Empowered Survival waved. "I think he's coming over," Lincoln mumbled. Nadia turned away, partially hiding her face. Several of the people in Rick Feldman's group turned toward them, and chatter broke out in the crowd.

"Fan-fucking-tastic," Perry groaned.

Rick approached with a beaming smile and clapped him on the shoulder. "We keep running into each other! Since when do you stay at a fancy hotel like this one, Perry? I heard about what happened to Clyde. I figured you'd cancel." He stuck out a hand for a handshake.

Perry smiled tightly, putting his hands in his pockets. "I'm sure you hoped I would."

"You know better than that. I'm rooting for you. And, who do we have here? Is this your little class?"

"That *is* him!" someone behind Rick gasped.

"Oh, my gosh! Lincoln Easley!" another woman shrieked.

"Lincoln! Lincoln!"

Lincoln smiled bashfully and backed away as a surge of people in the lobby rushed toward him. He took perverse pleasure in the dumbfound look on Rick's face. Served him right for his condescending tone with Perry. Lincoln put up his hands to ward off the more enthusiastic fans as Rick tried to call for order. "Alright, alright! Calm down!" Rick growled at his group.

Perry shook his head and chuckled. "Yeah, Rick. This is my *little* class. Sometimes less is more."

"One at a time," Lincoln stated. "I can only sign autographs one at a time."

"Need paper?" Perry reached in his pocket and pulled out a thick stack of business cards. Lincoln grinned, taking a pen from the front desk. It was genius. He scribbled his name on back of Perry's cards while Rick stood aside and scowled. Finally, Perry tapped his watch, and Lincoln nodded. They were on a schedule after all.

"That's all I can do for today, guys. Don't forget to check out *Vengeance with a Vengeance* in theaters now, and tell all your friends you met Lincoln Easley at Survive Anything," Lincoln announced.

"Well, that was worth the price of admission, thanks." Perry said quietly as he dragged him away.

Nadia reappeared behind them. "Did you have to make a scene?" she hissed.

Lincoln shrugged self-consciously. "I wasn't trying to make a scene. I was trying not to be rude. That would have been bad for my image."

"Yeah, well, I have an image to protect, too," Nadia complained. "Next time you want to be the center of attention, make sure I'm not around. No one needs to know I'm traveling into the woods with two strange men."

"Relax. Your reputation is safe with me. Let's get a move on," said

Perry. They quickly checked out of the hotel and exited the building, marching across the chilly parking lot. Perry climbed into the driver's seat of his Jeep and paused. "Before we go, I want to formally apologize for last night. It was an egregious lapse of judgement on my part, and I have no excuse for my behavior. I'm sorry."

"No apology necessary," Lincoln mumbled.

Perry glanced at him in the rearview mirror, and Lincoln went silent. The instructor continued, "It's vital that we reestablish the boundary between teacher and student, because I want this three-week course to be as worthwhile as possible —Christ, I don't even have a script for this."

"You don't need a script." Nadia said from the passenger seat. "Look, I think we're all on the same page, Perry. Like you said last night, it never happened. It's in all our best interest to run with that line."

Perry relaxed. "Good. We have a thirty-minute drive ahead of us. Once we arrive at the cabin, we'll get settled in and tackle our first objective. There's a lot to learn in a limited amount of time, and, I stress, there are risks involved. That's why it's so necessary to get back to you doing as I say without question or hesitation. We're not friends here."

"You know, there is a middle ground. We can be friends and still follow your leadership," Lincoln suggested.

Perry chuckled dryly. "We're not friends because I don't do friends, Lincoln Easley."

"Last night says different," Lincoln quipped. Perry smirked and powered on the radio. As he cranked the engine, Lincoln sighed. This was the point of no return. If he abandoned the training course now, Jasper Kent would take the lead in Mitch Trepan's next film, and Lincoln would never forgive himself. He had to put his desires on the back burner.

Nadia stared out the window with a rapt expression. "It's otherworldly," she whispered. Lincoln followed her line of sight to take his mind off the undercurrents swirling around in the truck. The landscape was, indeed, like something from an untouched planet. It was a breathtaking, welcome distraction, and it made him wish he had his phone so that he could at least take some pictures.

Lincoln suddenly had an idea. He dug his sketchbook and pencil colors out of his carry-on bag. His hand flew over the crisp white paper, recreating the world outside. The Blue Ridge Mountains kissed the early morning sky. The peaks were swathed in mist, and the mountains were a deep bluish purple underneath. Bare trees clung to rocky hillsides, evidence of approaching winter.

During his career, Lincoln had been to some of the most exotic places on earth, but he was often oblivious to his surroundings because of the never-ending demands of his vocation. This trip into the woods was a taste of what he had been missing. No lines to practice or blocking to choreograph. No cool, impersonal staff members. No pretenses to keep up.

Lincoln's eyes darted from the sketchbook to the mountains and he continued drawing. In a place like this, he could be free. Take last night, stripped of any need to perform, he had been himself. He remembered Perry's hands on him—his kiss, his taste. He remembered the exquisite perfection of Nadia's body. The silky fires of Perry's hand on his cock and the burning rapture of Nadia's sex tightening around him.

He shifted in the backseat to hide his erection and willed himself to stop thinking about the previous evening. Lascivious sex scenes with strangers came with the territory of being a Hollywood actor but Lincoln jealously guarded his personal life. He dated regular girls. He had a few one-night stands. Things occasionally got wild but last night was something else. For one thing, he most certainly had never been with a man.

He had kicked his usual reserved behavior to the curb in favor of letting Nadia take the lead, and she had led them straight to ecstasy. Now, a pact was made to pretend last night never happened. Lincoln wondered how long that would last.

He had a sneaking suspicion none of them were being completely honest about what they expected to occur once they made it to the cabin.

CHAPTER 6

T he winding mountain road was narrow and had hair-pin turns that appeared to dive right off the side. As the Jeep climbed higher, Nadia felt her ears pop. She cringed into the passenger seat, no longer interested in looking out the window. On her side of the vehicle was the stony mountain; on Perry's side was a steep drop to the wilderness below. "How much farther?" she gulped.

Perry casually drove with one hand, unfazed. "Scared of heights?" he asked with a grin. "Don't worry. We're almost there."

Nadia met his gaze. His mesmerizing blue eyes were steady, calm. She found a smile for him as he anchored her to the earth.

"When we get to basecamp, we'll go over some safety precautions before I take you into the woods," Perry explained. "Each core lesson spans one week, with the first one being the hardest, but it does get easier after that. We'll go out into the woods with nothing but the clothes on our backs and a knife."

Nadia's nervousness returned with a vengeance. "Has anyone ever gotten seriously injured out here with you?"

"Not once in the three years I've been doing this."

"You must be really good at what you do."

Perry chuckled. "I told you not to worry. You're in good hands."

Good hands, she thought. Last night those hands had been all over her body. This morning her father had reminded her that—even in the remotest locations—she had to refrain from doing anything scandalous. Perry's good hands would have to stay in their proper place from now on.

They arrived at the cabin that belonged to Perry's friend Clyde MacAskill, who was currently laid up at the hospital. Nadia had envisioned a cozy little hut, but the spacious two-story house boasted five bedrooms and a sitting room with a daybed. Every modern amenity was present, even a hot tub.

"Girl's gotta have her hot tub." Nadia beamed as she toured the house.

"Don't get comfortable. We won't be here long." Perry ushered his two students to the kitchen table and pulled a folder from his satchel, handing out papers to each of them.

"What's this?" Lincoln asked. Under the table, his foot absently stroked hers. His attention was on Perry's instructions, but the casual touch sent butterflies fluttering through her.

Nadia tried to focus. "I didn't expect literal classwork," she said as she scanned the top sheet, which outlined basic safety precautions.

"We'll get some hands-on experience for the stuff that requires it, but a lot of what I have to teach you is based in critical thinking." Perry lounged against the kitchen peninsula, a quirky half-smile tugging at his lips in a way that reminded her of what his mouth could do.

Focus, focus, focus, Nadia chanted inwardly. One of the documents was a checklist of items every family should have on stand-by in case of disaster. It included practical things like nutrient-rich nonperishables, first aid kits, tools and weaponry. Her father would be proud of Perry's attention to detail. *Maybe I should propose that he hires him instead of me.*

"I also emailed this to you when you signed up for the class. That covers that. Now," said Perry as he handed them wicked looking hunting knives, "any health issues I need to know about before we make our trek into the woods?"

Nadia considered mentioning she was operating on high arousal, which might complicate her ability to think clearly. She bit back a smile and shook her head in response to his question, though. "I sent you a copy of my history and physical from my primary care physician."

"Me, too," said Lincoln. "I'm excited to get going."

"Then, let's make it happen. You guys take a guest room and leave your belongings upstairs. Get dressed in your course-approved gear and meet me back here in five minutes."

"Special request?" Lincoln asked hopefully.

Perry crossed his arms. "We'll see. What is it?"

Lincoln held up his sketchbook. Nadia clasped her hands together, pleading, "Yeah! One notebook and pen or pencil each. Please? I promised my friend I would write to her."

"And since you trashed my phone, the only way I have to preserve these beautiful sights is through my drawing," Lincoln pointed out.

"Fine," Perry sighed. "Just know you won't be starting any fires with paper. Everything else about this survival training course is going by *my* book. Understand?"

Nadia and Lincoln's buoyant excitement carried them on a comfortable stroll along a well-worn path behind Clyde's cabin. The chilly air filled her lungs, but the warm layers of clothing kept her comfortable, and hiking boots made the walk easier. She drank in the experience.

The strong scent of evergreens made her think of Perry's cologne. Birdsong was punctuated by rustles in the underbrush and the buzz of insects, and a light breeze swirled thin, wispy fog that hung low. About a mile from base camp, Perry directed their attention to the sound of running water.

"You hear that? That's life," he said. "We want to build shelter near a water source."

He showed them how to make a round-lodge by using their knives to cut flexible green saplings that were about thumb thick. It was time-consuming, labor intensive work, but Nadia was pleased with herself for keeping up with the men. They assembled the long wood into a rounded conical shape attached to thicker bows and tied together with cord that Perry showed them how to make with dry grass.

It would take days to make enough cord to assemble the structure; so, after he taught them how to make the binding, he retrieved ready-made lengths of cord from his backpack and helped them use it to bring the round-lodge together. Once done, they insulated the lower half of the building with mud and grass from the streambed.

By the time construction was complete, the sun had sunk beneath the tree line, and the clearing was cold. Perry beckoned for Nadia to step into the shelter with him. Her eyes widened in surprise. "It's warmer in here."

"Mm-hm. It'll be even warmer once the three of us are in here together."

"This is amazing."

"Shelters like these were predominantly used by early settlers in the Midwest. It's a strong design that will provide temporary shelter in nearly any situation until you can build something sturdier. Told you that you were in good hands."

Nadia conceded that she trusted him. Their eyes locked, and Perry hesitantly touched her cheek with the pad of his thumb. She licked her lips as the heat in the room went up another few degrees. The spell was broken when Lincoln stepped into the spacious lodge. "What's next, boss?"

"Now, we learn how to build a fire."

Nadia whispered to herself, "I thought we covered that lesson last night."

Lincoln blushed, but Perry ignored the comment. They used friction build-up, rubbing two sticks together to ignite a carefully constructed fire pit. Nadia pouted when Lincoln mastered the task quickly while she struggled to get the hang of it.

"Take your time. This isn't a race," Perry murmured.

"He's done this before."

"Yeah, I was a Boy Scout," Lincoln acknowledged.

"See!"

Perry grinned and shook his head. "So what? Does that mean you shouldn't learn how? Stop being a spoiled brat and keep trying." Within minutes, the blazing fire warmed the clearing around the round-lodge, and the heat radiated to the shelter where Nadia sat down to rest. "Aren't you proud of yourself?"

"I'm not spoiled," she grumbled.

"You are, but that's okay. We're all products of our environment."

"Shade thrown?"

"Not at all. My point is, we're sculpted by our challenges. Challenge yourself, even if no one else is challenging you. When you step back and see what you've accomplished with your own two hands, you gain the confidence to do more. Now that we've got a shelter and a fire going, what's the next priority?" Perry asked.

"Food and water," Lincoln answered immediately. His stomach growled audibly. The hard work of building a shelter had taken a lot out of them.

Perry reached into his backpack and brought out three large fabric canteens. "We can't hunt tonight, but we can forage, and, tomorrow, I'll teach you how to make these." He dropped the canteens inside their shelter. "Nadia, you need a break? Lincoln, come with me. Let's go see what we can find to eat."

"Ugh! I think I'm losing some of my enthusiasm for this," he complained with a laugh.

Nadia chuckled and moved closer to the fire. "No, I can help, you guys. I'm *not* the weakest link."

"It doesn't take three people to forage. If you want to help, I can show you how to make a bough bed. Let's get the frames in place. Then, you can fill it with dry leaves and grass. You'll want to make the mattress about six inches thick to get us off the ground and provide insulation against the cold. Can you handle it?"

"We'll see," she replied. That smoky quality tinged her voice again.

~

Perry found downed branches that were large enough to provide the frame of the bed, and Lincoln lugged them with him to the shelter despite the fact that his muscles ached and his blood sugar was crashing. He could not wait to get back to civilization to give Mitch Trepan a piece of his mind. What made the director think this experience was what he needed to be a better actor?

His hands were dirty and blistered from sawing through boughs all afternoon. He was sweaty. He hated to think of what he would smell like after a few more days of this. Lincoln blew out a frustrated sigh as Perry gestured for him to join him foraging for food.

"Why would anyone want to do this?" Lincoln muttered. "With all the technological advances we have, this is work for the sake of work. And what the hell is on the forager menu?"

"Weeds, roots and bark. Berries, if we're lucky."

"What about protein?"

"Pick a rock. I'll show you the best grubs and larvae you can find," Perry chuckled.

"Please tell me you're pulling my leg!"

"You'll eat anything you have to, if you get hungry enough." Perry led him closer to the stream where the waning light fell upon nothing that looked remotely edible. "You have to know where to look. You don't want anything from the roadside or anything that might have been exposed to dangerous pollutants and pesticides. Forage from places with low traffic, like out here."

They found dandelion and chicory, wild leeks and elderberry and returned to camp with the bounty of "food." Nadia was still working on the beds. Perry used a flat stone slab and made a salad. Finally, the three of them settled close to the fire and ate together.

The greens were bitter, but the elderberries were sweet and tart. Perry lauded the benefits of eating clean. Nadia tentatively tried everything laid before her as her expression ranged from perplexed to bravely determined. Lincoln found the meal barely palatable, and his stomach begged for real food. "This feels like a punishment." He tried to force a laugh, but was obviously struggling to find the humor in the situation.

With a grin, Perry gestured back the way they had come. "The moss grows on the north side of the tree. If you don't like how I do things around here, you're welcome to make your way north to the cabin."

"You're getting a kick out of this, aren't you?" Lincoln accused. Something about Perry's smug grin made him angrier. The survival instructor spread his arms and shrugged.

"I'm just giving you your options. You can eat this, go hungry, or go home."

Nadia's eyes swung from Perry to Lincoln.

"And I'm just saying," Lincoln fired back, "you could offer protein bars or something. It'll do your business some good. You've got us eating weeds like nut jobs. I mean, you don't like Rick Feldman, but I saw his brochure. Whatever *he's* doing is working."

Perry's jaw tightened perceptibly, but he spoke calmly. "Oh, thanks for the business advice. Better yet, you can quit now and sign up for Rick's course. See where that gets you." Perry chuckled bitterly and shook his head. "You don't take this seriously anyway. For you, this is about a character you'll be playing in a movie."

"Oh, come on! I don't take this seriously?'" Lincoln exclaimed defensively.

Perry pinned him with a look. "I'm not here to entertain you or to stroke your ego. I'm here to teach you how to have a chance at making it in a dangerous world. So, my offer still stands. You don't like how I run things? Get the fuck out of my camp!"

"Guys," Nadia interjected. She swept her hands through the air in a slicing motion. "Enough with the pissing match. We're in this together."

Lincoln backed down. He hated to seem like a jerk, but Perry was pushing his buttons. He wondered if things would have gotten as heated if they had not slept together. The argument was laced with tensions from sexual frustration, a desire to dominate, a need to regain control of a situation none of them seemed to have control over.

"You're right," he sighed. "We're in this together." Lincoln stuck out a conciliatory hand which Perry pointedly ignored.

CHAPTER 7

Perry came to a creek that was glistening in the moonlight, found a sizeable boulder and took a seat at the water's edge. He was off his game, acting out of character.

He found Lincoln's lack of curiosity unsettling. Even Nadia's complaints about building a fire had grated on his nerves. The same qualities that were good for publicity—Lincoln and Nadia's fame and fortune—would make it difficult for Perry to show them he had something of merit to offer.

"This is my life," he whispered to himself. He taught survival skills because he was a survivor. Of course, Nadia and Lincoln were having trouble adapting to his world. Maybe it was his fault. Perry rarely connected with people, much preferring his own company.

They had, however, shown him a good time at the hotel and made him hopeful this trip would be fun. Maybe that was why he was taking this so damn personally. Perry sighed and skipped a stone. It plunked into the water and he sighed again in frustration. To get through these three weeks with his sanity intact, he would have to stop imagining what could be and accept what was. The others were way out of his league and nothing was going to change that.

Perry heard footsteps behind him. Lincoln settled next to him and stared out at the water. "I didn't mean to set you off," Lincoln muttered.

"The other day," said Perry, "Rick Feldman made a jab about the spike in sign-ups during uncertain times, but I understand why people do that. Terrorism, war or natural disasters, make some people scared. Most look to authority for help and reassurance but a small subset of people get into radical self-reliance. I'm trying to teach you how to be radically self-reliant."

"I appreciate it. Perry, I wasn't trying to offend you or make light of your passion. I'm just not the kind of guy to build a bunker in my backyard. I mean, I get that anything can happen at any time, but I don't jump at every conspiracy theory. I'm not that paranoid."

Perry nodded, understanding that, too. "I'm not talking about paranoia. I'm talking about emergency preparedness. The average American believes our society is set, ad infinitum. Our money will always be good. Our government will always be benevolent. And our neighbors will always stay on their side of the fence. But that's an illusion."

He looked at Lincoln. "After Hurricane Katrina, you know a lot of sick and injured people were stuck in a large metropolitan area without access to food water or the most basic of services. Power grids went out, waste management systems went down, and this lead to a whole host of problems. Let me ask you this: You carry a lot of cash on you?"

"No," Lincoln snorted. "That'd be asking to be robbed."

"Yeah? How do you get access to the money in your bank when the roads are washed out and the ATMs don't work? Hurricane Katrina happened over a decade ago. We're even more dependent on the power grids and internet now. Ever thought of that?"

Lincoln chuckled quietly and rubbed his hands together slowly. "I'm thinking about it now."

Perry stared at his hands. Large, elegant hands that would get calluses and chipped fingernails over the next few weeks. Perry wanted to lace their fingers together, but he restrained himself.

They both looked back when Nadia approached, hugging herself to ward against the cold. "I come in peace," she said lightheartedly.

Perry smiled and beckoned her to join them. "I'm sorry for being temperamental. I think Lincoln and I see eye to eye now. We were just talking about radical self-reliance and the state of the world."

"My father and some of his friends talk about it all the time. They have a survivalist club. I think that's why he hasn't put up much fuss about me being here," she said. Perry kept his thoughts to himself and nodded for her to continue. "We have an insurance home in New Zealand. In the event of wide scale societal collapse, we have a safe-haven. I used to think Dad was being over the top, but lately I consider it forward-thinking."

"Is it forward-thinking?" Perry asked lightly. "I imagine it's a step backwards."

"Why so?"

He did not answer. He did not want to get into a spirited debate about how billionaires could afford to invest in fixing the problems instead of running from them. *He wanted to kiss her.* Perry forced the thought away. Rising to his feet, he gestured toward camp where the fire was dying.

"I think we better get more firewood before it gets late. Nadia, why don't you grab the canteens and take water back to camp. We'll meet you there."

"Wait! Why do you think it's a step backwards?"

"Because," he sighed. "The same things that destroy the world will be waiting in the hearts of men, no matter how many utopias we try to build. You can run, but you can't hide from human nature." The words rang in his head as he ambled away with Lincoln on his heels. Back at the hotel, Nadia had called the volatile chemistry between them human nature. They could not hide from that, either.

～

I n the days that followed, Lincoln managed to keep his complaints to a minimum, and time passed. Each day, there was so much to learn, so much to do, that by nightfall the three of them fell into bed, exhausted.

They developed a regular routine, rising early and washing up with water from the creek. For soap, Perry extracted tannins from aspen bark boiled in a hollowed-out rabbit skull. The astringent, murky black solution was great for bathing.

They each had two sets of clothes and when one outfit got dirty, they washed it and hung it on the trees to dry. It was not a perfect system, but it worked. Perry taught them how to groom without conventional tools of hygiene. They used a chewed and softened sassafras twig to brush their teeth using a primitive toothpaste made from ashes.

Around the third day out, Perry appeared with a bristly plant that he held up proudly. "Found this. Teasel plant. It's an invasive species that normally isn't cultivated, but it grows wild. If we get rid of all the seedpods, this will make a perfect hairbrush," he announced.

He later produced a medicinal stash of homemade alcohol and taught them how to make neem-infused insect-repellant when Nadia complained about the bugs. Using the tip of a knife, he showed them resin bubbles on a spruce tree and pierced each pocket to produce enough resin for her bites. The clear, antibacterial sap was perfect for wound healing.

Perry also showed them how to make deodorant in the wilderness, explaining that it was not a vital survival component. They picked usnea, a pale green lichen, from the branches of a spruce tree. He demonstrated how to moisten their underarms with water from the creek and how to rub sun-dried usnea along the skin to minimize body odor.

Breakfast was whatever they could forage, trap, fish or hunt. Lincoln developed an appreciation for the peaceful nature walks they took to gather food. He enjoyed the playful banter that belied the simmering attraction that smoldered just under the surface. They grew closer and became good friends, no matter how hard Perry tried to keep the barriers in place.

With every bush-craft lesson, Perry's calming voice stirred arousal. He would put a hand over Lincoln's to show him proper form or stand close behind him and whisper instructions. At night, Nadia would gravitate toward him like the moon caught in earth's pull. Lincoln would wrap his arms around her and breathe in the scent of her sweat and think it was better than any perfume money could buy.

He had no clue whether his senses simply grew accustomed to less luxury and frills or if his primal nature was unleashed by the setting. The hard work of surviving day to day left Lincoln aching for sex. Whenever the desire became too strong to ignore, he would slip away from camp and sketch to take his mind off the tantalizing fantasies.

He caught himself staring when he had no reason to stare, daydreaming when he should have been focused on work. Nadia, who had seemed most eager to flaunt social conventions in the beginning, now seemed determined to keep the men at arm's length. Perry, for his part, was diligent about maintaining a proper student/teacher relationship.

Lincoln seemed to be the only one suffering from flashbacks of their one-night stand. He wondered what would happen when the days wound down and they had to go back to their real lives. He filled his sketchbook with memories, knowing it was all he would take with him when he went back to Hollywood.

As the week closed out on Friday night, he looked forward to next, when they would move on to another camp. Then, he could expend his excess energy on the hike. Anything to take the edge off.

Nadia scooted closer to the warm, crackling campfire. The cold air was laden with the smell of the roasted rabbit the three of them had enjoyed just moments earlier. She licked her lips and gazed at the cold blue-black sky. She looked back down at the letter she was writing to Maria.

With Lincoln and Perry away getting more firewood, she had time to herself to think of the unlikely bond forming between the three of them, and her thoughts tumbled onto the page:

I have a confession to make. My notebook is filling with letters I've written to you that I'll deliver as soon as I get back to Perry's cabin. (No mail service in the woods.) But there's an issue I've been skirting around, with all my talk of what I've seen and learned on this trip.

Firstly, you and I both know I'm going through a rebellious phase. I never expected to go through this in adulthood, but I guess that's what happens when you play by the rules all through middle school, high school and college.

When everyone else was sneaking cigarettes and leaving the club with strangers, I was hitting the books hard and trying to make my daddy proud.

Now, how bad does it look that I'm damn near twenty-seven and still acting like this? I know what you'll say. You'll say I'm an adult, and I'm allowed. I've been telling myself the same thing for the past week. I just wonder how much of this is about positive exploration and how much is escapism.

The only reason I came out here was to run away from Marson Oil and Gas. My dad thinks I'm nervous about taking the job, but the truth—as you know—is that I just don't want it. And the problem is that I don't know what I do want.

Anyway, when I tell you this, you have to promise me that you won't judge me. I mean, I know you won't. You never do. When I told you how badly I made a fool of myself behind Jason Stratham, you were ready to hop a plane to California to kick his ass for me. But this is different.

Maria, I had a three—

Dry kindling clattered to the ground beside her, and Nadia jumped and slammed her notebook shut. "Back already? I was just writing a letter to Maria—my, uh, my best friend. I met her in that hurricane I mentioned. Something about danger that makes people bond…" She realized she was rambling and bit her lip in an attempt to stop talking.

Lincoln eyed her in amusement as he sat near the fire. "Sounds exciting. Telling her about us?"

"Don't be ridiculous," Nadia laughed nervously. "I've tangoed with gossip rags before. Some secrets are best taken to the grave." *You hear that, self?* She shoved her notebook under the leaves of her bough bed and returned to the fire just as Perry brought out the moonshine.

"Since it's Friday night, I figured the three of us could celebrate making it through the first week of training. Congratulations! You've earned yourself Mason jars to go with your hunting knives," he said with a grin.

"About these gossip rags," Lincoln persisted. "You've been in the tabloids, Nadia?"

Nadia cringed, reliving the ugly memory. "Six months ago, my ex-boyfriend cheated on me with a reality TV star who shall not be named. You probably know her. We tried to keep the breakup low profile. Unfortunately, the details got out, and I had to stare at crying pictures of myself on the front cover of National Enquirer for weeks. Part of the reason I ran off to the islands was to get away from the coverage."

"That's where you went through the hurricane?"

She nodded. "I learned two things from that experience: One, be prepared for anything, and, two, don't give them anything to talk about. Damn my ex."

"Hear, hear." Perry handed her a Mason jar and filled it halfway with clear, smooth corn liquor.

"Jason Stratham will think twice before he cheats on someone else," she said as she took a generous sip. "When you mess with a Marson, you take on the whole empire."

Lincoln laughed heartily. "You are something else, Ms. Nadia Marson, a force to be reckoned with. He had to be an idiot to cheat on you."

"Trying to butter me up, Lincoln? Flattery will get you every-where. I was the bigger idiot," Nadia admitted. "I stuck with Jason, even though I knew he was all wrong for me. It took the paparazzi to get me to wake up and come to my senses. I've been single ever since. Maybe that's why all of this has happened."

"All of what?" Perry met her gaze.

She giggled and waved her arms to encompass the waning campfire and the three of them. "Oh, you know! Tumbling into bed with you guys. It's not like me. I'm typically a very boring person."

"I can think of a number of ways to describe you, but 'boring' doesn't make the list."

Nadia shrugged and focused her attention on her drink. The hooch was cold and crisp but had an instant warming effect. The heat started in her chest. Or perhaps somewhere in her pelvis. She squirmed. "It's better to be boring, Perry. If anyone finds out what we did, they'll run with the story. That's why I didn't want to be seen at the hotel with you guys."

"It's nobody's business what we do out here," Perry topped off her glass.

Nadia knew she should say no to alcohol, but she accepted extra with a smile. "Nobody's business what we do out here? Is that an invitation?"

"I'm just saying...Hypothetically speaking, even if some crazy tabloid investigator braved the elements to get the scoop on what we're doing in the woods, you two could easily deny it," said Perry. "I wouldn't want to be rich or famous. I prefer my privacy. But I know a thing or two about speculation, and what people *think* is going on doesn't matter if they can't prove it."

"You still haven't answered my question," Nadia said carefully. "Is that an invitation?"

CHAPTER 8

"Do you want it to be?" Perry asked. The camp was quiet, save for the sound of the crackling fire. Lincoln looked from Perry to Nadia, feeling the temperature rise between the three of them. All week, they had kept their desires in check, but it was the end of the first stage, and the alcohol was flowing freely. With one simple question, their best efforts at feigning indifference was shot to pieces.

Lincoln wanted Nadia to give the go-ahead, to move one step beyond the tease and give voice to what he was thinking. *Why keep up the charade?* He was tired of pretending. They were so far away from civilization that they could do whatever they wanted to do. Social norms were irrelevant, what people thought of them was irrelevant.

He took a hasty swallow of moonshine and felt the fiery spirit burn its way through his chest as Nadia shrugged noncommittally. "My father warned me to protect my reputation," she said finally. Lincoln's shoulders slumped. "But..."

Nadia let the statement trail off, but she knew that Lincoln and Perry were waiting with bated breath. Lincoln knew his emotions were written plainly, while the survival instructor kept a poker face. "Well?" he prompted.

Nadia wordlessly lifted her thermal shirt and drew it over her head, revealing a black tank top. Her full breasts strained the cotton fabric, and Lincoln's arousal ticked up several notches. "Well, what they can't prove won't hurt us, right?" Nadia whispered.

Perry restlessly ran a hand over his abs, as if still trying to hold himself back. She unfastened her fatigues and let the pants fall to the ground, and he lost the battle. "Get in the round lodge. You'll catch a chill," he ordered.

Lincoln quickly pushed to his feet and opened the door to the lodge for her. Nadia brushed past him, her excitement palpable. He could almost taste it. He filed into the lodge, and Perry stepped in behind him and shut them away from the rest of the world. The heat from the campfire permeated the enclosure, providing enough warmth in the shelter for Nadia to completely undress.

She was naked and vulnerable between them. She laid a hand over Lincoln's crotch, and his manhood lengthened and hardened in response. She eased Perry's erection from his pants and slowly masturbated him. Then, she freed Lincoln's cock and brought the men together. It was different and erotic. Perry's rigid shaft probed his. Lincoln bit back a moan.

"Is it bad that I want both of you?" she asked thoughtfully.

"No," he sighed. He wanted them both, too. The lodge filled with the sound of heavy breathing as she leaned forward and drizzled a silky web of spit over their erections. Lincoln let his head drop back in wonder.

With a groan, Perry cupped him by the neck, and Lincoln stumbled closer, throwing his arms around the buff survival instructor to catch his balance. They kissed feverishly as he ripped off Perry's shirt and shrugged out of his own. Nadia slid to her knees and unbuckled his fatigues.

In seconds, her mouth was on his swollen cock and his sounds of pleasure were muffled by Perry's hungry lips. They flowed seamlessly to the bed of leaves. Gone was the reticence of the first time. The taxing week of self-restraint went up in flames, and they eagerly touched, kissed and explored each other.

"Tell me I'm not the only one whose been dying to do this," Lincoln sputtered.

"You're not," Nadia swore. On hands and knees, she shifted her attention to Perry. Her dark hair curtained her face as she lowered her mouth to his erection. He sucked in a breath, and his face tightened with ecstasy.

"No, I tried," Perry hissed. "I tried to keep this from happening, but I can't. Still, this changes nothing! I'm in charge of—Oh, fuck, Nadia!" She took him deeper into her mouth, rendering them both speechless.

Perry rode her face slow and hard. Lincoln watched the X-rated scene play out with throbbing anticipation. He watched the way Perry brushed her hair back from her face and stared at her with unconcealed appreciation. The way his lips parted in a muted scream, and his eyelids fluttered from the rapturous oral sex.

He was unbelievably beautiful, but so was she. Nadia's body danced sinuously as her head rose and fell. Lincoln could not resist touching her. He palmed her tight snatch, slipping his middle finger into her slick, wet heat. As she rocked against his hand, she emitted wanton sighs of excitement, and his manhood hardened painfully.

Lincoln shed the rest of his clothes as he repositioned behind her. He spread her buttocks and placed his mouth over her dewy lower lips, eating her out as she rocked on hands and knees. Her intoxicating scent filled his nostrils.

Her pussy advanced and retreated, and he dipped his tongue into her copious nectar, fucking her with the pliable spear. The wicked act seemed to trigger something wild and uninhibited within her. She trembled and jerked in rapture. Her plaintive cries increased in volume. "Mm, give it all to me!" he hummed greedily.

Nadia reached back and gripped a fistful of his wavy hair. He caressed her clit with the tip of his tongue, letting her guide his face. He closed his mouth over her pulsating erogenous zone. Her cries grew even louder, echoing in the night. As her excitement climbed, so did Perry's. The survival trainer clutched her shoulders and raked his blunt nails over her back, struggling for self-control.

"You have to stop," Perry warned. Nadia whimpered in disagreement. "Fuck! You're amazing, but you have to stop." Perry forcefully pushed her away. Spasms roiled through his massive cock as if he was milliseconds from blowing his load. Lincoln stared at the fat purple tip, mesmerized. Perry clutched himself, shuddering.

"Come here," Lincoln whispered to their princess. He grabbed her under her knees and dragged her into position. Her long, curvy legs parted for him. Dipping the spear of his tongue into the folds of her pussy, he licked his way to her pounding clit and sucked. With rhythmic pulls of his lips and tongue, he tantalized her to madness.

"Lincoln!" she cried out breathlessly.

Right there, he thought. He was in the right place. He penetrated her body with two probing fingers and let his tongue sweep over her clit. Up and down, faster. He probed and prodded her G-spot while he tasted her. "Give it up for me," he whispered.

"Oh, God! Lincoln!" She bucked against his mouth.

He was so focused on his task that he did not notice Perry until the sexy military vet gently nudged him from behind. Lincoln glanced over his shoulder in surprise. "Perry...?"

"No! Don't stop!" Nadia trembled beneath him and cried out. She writhed in Lincoln's arms, and her pelvis jerked forward to meet his mouth. Lincoln gave her his attention even as he tried to attend to what Perry was doing.

"Just breathe," Perry whispered.

Lincoln felt slick, warm liquid spill down the crease of his ass. "Careful," he gasped as Perry eased a finger inside of him. Along with the stinging pain came tingling anticipation. He was scared, but he was eager. Nadia mindlessly clasped his face to her body and grinded against his mouth in climax, and Perry dominated his imagination with the in and out press of his digit.

It loosened him for more. This is what you wanted, Lincoln told himself. His mouth went dry as he tried to prepare for what would come next. When Perry rose on his knees and placed the blunt tip of his cock to his entrance, he was as ready as he would ever be. The first attempt shot daggers of shock through his system. Lincoln tensed and cried out. But Nadia sat forward and brushed her mouth over his, tasting her essence on his lips.

"Shh...relax," she whispered soothingly. Her hands smoothed over his forehead and swept around to the back of his neck as she locked eyes with him. "You can stop at any point. If it gets too intense, say the word."

Lincoln nodded. He thought about all the dates he had gone on just to make someone happy, all the pretending he had done in Hollywood. He thought, strangely, of Carmen, whom he had turned down on the set of *Vengeance with a Vengeance* in a rare authentic moment when he had not felt like keeping up appearances. Then, he remembered how it had felt to let go at the hotel with Nadia and Perry.

This was the moment he had been waiting for, another chance to be himself completely. This was what Lincoln wanted, and it would take crossing this threshold to get it again. He squeezed his eyes shut and exhaled, letting the tension flow from his body. He felt Perry stroke himself along the seam of his ass and whispered, "I'm ready."

Perry's arm snaked over the plane of his hip to anchor him in place. He pressed forward with slow, steady determination as he soaked Lincoln's asshole with more spit. The extra lubricant eased the transition. Lincoln's neck turned vibrant red as he received him inch by inch.

Perry groaned. His erection surged past the tightest stricture, and Lincoln whined softly as the discomfort turned to something different—something wet and unexpected. He was stunned by the pleasure. It hit out of the blue and flamed through him like wildfire.

"Perry," he gasped.

"Yes! Oh! Yes!" Perry shuddered. The momentum of his excitement powered through his hips. He pushed deeper into Lincoln's body, thighs bunching. They slammed together. He grabbed a fistful of Lincoln's hair and pulled him back to arch his spine as he fucked him harder.

Lincoln clamped his bottom lip between his teeth. When he opened his eyes, he saw Nadia touching herself. Her seductive stare heightened the moment. She turned around and lay on her stomach in an inviting pose. Lincoln fell forward on top of her.

With her legs together, he straddled her ass and guided his erection past the hills of her derriere. He found the valley of her pussy and thrust his throbbing dick into her body, and her mouth dropped open in a hoarse scream of ecstasy.

Her pillowy soft pussy enveloped him from tip to base, and he clutched her closer. She fucked him like her survival depended on it. Her heart-shaped ass jiggled with every spirited bounce. There was something about her reactions that made him lose control. It was the wild hair or the excitement on her face, her pink lips sobbing his name.

Perry's determined strokes propelled Lincoln back and forth, like Perry was fucking them both. Lincoln wrapped his forearm around Nadia's neck and nibbled her earlobe, panting against the side of her face with every delicious move.

All he could think was *more*. He wanted everything they had to give and more.

∿

Perry grabbed Lincoln by the hair and brought his face around for a steamy kiss. From this vantage point, he could watch Lincoln's reaction. But he could hardly focus on the grimace of ecstasy on his lover's face for marveling at his own rapture.

He spread Lincoln's ass cheeks and went balls deep. He felt like he would blast off any second. He looked down in amazement at where their bodies connected, and he listened to the sounds their bodies made as they slammed together.

His thick, corded cock plowed into Lincoln's receptive ass while Nadia writhed beneath him. The three of them rose and fell with fluid grace. The very thought of what they were doing was almost enough to make him come, but he held back.

He had never been intimate with a man, and the differences were stark. Instead of soft, yielding flesh, Lincoln's body was muscular and hard. His taut buttocks clenched around Perry's shaft, leaving him awestruck by the tightness sucking him deeper. The faster he plunged, the tighter Lincoln seemed to become.

In the back of his mind, Perry wondered if he would ever be the same after this. Nothing sexual had ever been this intense, and he doubted anything else would ever measure up. Growling, he rolled away. "Enough!"

"Gah!" Lincoln exhaled in a daze when he pulled out.

"You're so fucking good to me," Perry whispered, kissing him hungrily.

"Why'd you stop?"

"I'm gonna come."

"Is that a bad thing?" Lincoln grinned.

Perry chuckled and sat back, masturbating. "I'm not ready for this to end."

Nadia begged Lincoln to keep going, and he flipped her on her back and eagerly rubbed her clit as he pushed inside again. Perry watched her tight sheath clench around Lincoln's pulsing dick. He could see her juices dribbling down. He spit on his hand and stroked himself faster as Lincoln squeezed her breasts, turning him on even more.

Lincoln rose over her and pushed her legs back, putting one calf over his shoulder. He rocked slow and hard, and she moved sinuously to meet his thrusts. Perry reveled in the magic of her body. His lips parted in a tremulous exhale. Her wetness never seemed to dissipate. Perry slid a hand down her flat stomach and touched the hot, wet glory between her legs.

"Nadia, Nadia, Nadia...Do you feel like a bad girl?" His other hand sprinted up and down his stolid shaft, and the look in her eyes said they were fighting the same battle in the war not to come too soon. "Say you like it," Perry whispered. He caressed her face with the pad of his thumb. He stroked her lips with her creamy nectar. With a sultry moan, she captured his finger between her lips and sucked.

"Yes," Lincoln hissed. He held her by the hips and drilled her sexy body harder. The way she counter-thrust to meet him heightened

Perry's arousal. Lincoln grinded against her. His deep, powerful strokes sought only to go deeper, not to reemerge from her oasis. He scraped against her clit with every tension-filled rock of his hips.

Nadia wrapped her arm around Lincoln's neck and strained to meet him. His ass tightened as he pumped into her, and Perry smacked his tempting cheeks. He guided him in and out of Nadia's body as Lincoln stammered her name and pinned her to the ground, sinking deeper. Both were at the breaking point. It was bliss. It was indescribable to watch.

Suddenly, he wanted to be anywhere in between. He let his massive cock whisper over their lips, and they kissed around his erection, but Perry needed action. He desperately pushed into Lincoln's mouth, rushing to the back of his throat. Perry went weak in the knees when Lincoln sucked the tangy, sweet pre-cum from his cock.

Nadia took charge and masturbated him against her lips. He dove inside her mouth, ready to paint her face with his excitement. The harder Lincoln fucked her, the harder and faster she sucked him. Her muted cries of ecstasy met a crescendo, and suddenly her body gushed hot wetness around Lincoln's erection.

"Ooh, shit!" Perry whispered.

"Fuck! Nadia! Ah!" Lincoln gripped her hip, gripped a handful of her hair, pounded harder. Harder. He quickly fell back, vigorously stroking himself as his beautiful dick erupted in climax. And Perry moved over him and let his cock bathe in the downpour, knowing he was lost. He masturbated against Lincoln's soft, warm balls, feeling every spasm of his orgasm. Then, Perry squeezed his eyes shut and let go.

The veins stood out on his muscular biceps. His hips bucked and he whimpered loudly as jizz exploded from his cock and shot to his lover's glistening skin. Perry stroked the head of his cock in dizzying circles, watching the pearly white cum spill all over his and Lincoln's erections. Lincoln moaned his name and came into his arms, kissing him fervently. Nadia shifted closer, as well. Perry slid a hand between her legs to feel her heat.

As he regained composure, he realized how far from the path he had strayed. Letting primal instincts take charge, he had cut through the boundaries again. It might take days to restore order. He sighed in disappointment with himself. Nadia looked at him askance, but there was no way to explain that men like him did not form these kinds of bonds.

He was a loner by choice. He was a loner by nature. Why get involved with two other people who were just passing through his life? Sighing, he rose from the bed of leaves where they had just found bliss, and he grabbed his clothes. No one spoke as he redressed and stepped out to the cold dark night. The fire smoldered. He walked past it and disappeared into the woods. He went to the creek and washed the scent of sex from his body.

He sat by the water and contemplated how he was going to keep his business afloat. Because, if he let his lust get the best of him again, he would never accomplish his goals. The last thing he needed was for Nadia and Lincoln to feel forced to distance themselves from him after the retreat was over. Instead, he needed them to spread the word about Survive Anything. They had no idea he was the one who needed them to survive, and that made him feel like the worst kind of user.

CHAPTER 9

Dear *Maria,* Nadia wrote.

I'm sleeping with them. Yep, both of them. Who would have thought the key to my happiness would be not one, but two men? And don't worry about castigating me for my behavior. I've beat myself up enough, but my libido just refuses to pay attention!

It happened first at the hotel and then again over the weekend. You'll never guess the most titillating part. Lincoln and Perry are just as attracted to each other as they are to me. That should be a turn off, right? Only it isn't. These guys are alphas—assertive and dominant. Multiply the wet effect times two.

Anyway, I keep going back to the thought that my subconscious is using this to rebel against my father. Maybe that was the case in the beginning, but now I'm not so sure. There must be more to it than that.

I know that this could be the worst mistake of my life. I mean, Lincoln is a self-absorbed actor, and Perry is a moody ass military vet. In another two weeks, we'll say goodbye like this never even happened. This should never have gone this far. Yet, I can't say no to this.

They make me feel alive. That's what has me worried. What the hell am I going to feel like when this is all over?

She closed the notebook and slid it under the leaves of her bough bed. As she got up to exit the round lodge, she noticed Lincoln's sketchbook and flipped it open. What she saw stopped her dead in her tracks. There were breathtaking vistas that were stunning enough, but it was the way he had rendered Perry and herself that caught her off guard. She ran her fingers over a smooth sketch of her in profile. When the door to the lodge swung open, she guiltily closed the book.

"What are you doing?" Lincoln asked.

"I was—I just wanted to see your drawings."

"Curious about me, are you?" He grinned.

"I didn't say *that*."

"Actions speak louder than words. Come on out. Perry snared a squirrel for breakfast."

She wrinkled her nose and chuckled. "Man, I can't wait to get back to civilization."

He met her gaze as he grabbed her hand. "I can," he murmured. She understood the sentiment. Nadia sighed, thinking about the letter she had written to Maria. She was only allowed to cut free and break all the rules out here. When the trio got back to civilization, the joyride would be over.

She stepped into the clearing where the smell of roast meat filled the air, and her mouth began to water. Perry handed her a canteen. "We're hiking out today," he murmured.

She shot a glance at Lincoln, worried by Perry's flat tone. He lifted a shoulder in a shrug and shook his head. Last night, Perry had returned to the lodge and quietly gone to bed with no talk of what they had done. He still seemed to be in an introspective mood about it.

"Where are we going?" Nadia asked.

Perry finally cracked a smile. "This week, I have a special treat for you. We're heading higher into the mountains to visit the hot springs since health and wellbeing is on the lesson plan for the next few days."

"Are you serious?!" Nadia squealed excitedly.

"I figured you'd like that, but I do really need to lay out some ground rules before we go. Nadia, Lincoln, if we're going to keep sleeping together, it's only fair I tell you I'm not available for anything else after this. It's just...sex."

Nadia crossed her arms defensively. "Yeah, sure! What else would it be? I'd never bring a guy like you home. I have a reputation to protect."

Perry looked momentarily taken aback by her response. She wondered if her casual dismissal of him made him think of the time she had called him "staff" back at the hotel. But he smoothed his face and gestured at the campfire. "Wonderful. Glad we're on the same page. Now, let's eat, break camp and move on out."

They feasted on a hearty meal of squirrel and wild greens. The food settled like a lump of concrete in her stomach. It's just sex, he had said. Nadia knew his words were not personal, but maybe that was part of the problem.

After the meal, they meticulously scrubbed the clearing of any signs of their presence and packed their few belongings. Perry took them along a winding path through the woods. The ascent was gentle and not physically taxing in the least. This gave Nadia plenty of time to think.

Why had he felt the need to brush them off like that? She felt catty for suggesting he was subpar dating material, but why did it matter, when he clearly wanted them to know he was not interested in a relationship?

Nadia wondered what kind of internal war he was waging—a heterosexual male suddenly finding himself attracted to another man. It had to be doubly disconcerting for Perry, who seemed to place a high premium on all things macho. It was nobody's fault that they couldn't keep their hands off one another.

Whatever the reason for his distancing act, the walls were back up between the three of them. Lincoln had also pulled back and was every bit as emotionally distant as Perry. Nadia hated to admit it, but her feelings were hurt. She was stuck with a lust she could hardly control and zero prospects of a happily ever after.

After all, it really is just a bad case of 'in lust,' she told herself. She was a young woman with a bright future ahead of her that did not include running off with two strange men. Even if she wanted more, Perry was content with his isolation, and Lincoln came from a world that she wanted no part of. A world where sex was 'just sex.'

By the time they came upon their second encampment, she had made up her mind. She could handle ill-fated attraction. When the time came to part ways, she would be okay with it. After all, neither of these guys was in love with her. If anything, they thought *she* was risky dating material—wealthy, high-maintenance, and under her father's thumb to boot.

Hell, if she were in their position, she would run in the opposite direction, too. Nadia rolled up her sleeves in the brisk fall air and got to work helping Perry and Lincoln make another round lodge. She hid her blues well. On the bright side, at least she was getting a hot spring vacation out of the deal.

~

L incoln stretched, feeling limber and at peace as the sunset turned the mountainside a dark, misty blue. The first stars were out, and the baying of wolves in the distance came like a lullaby that no longer bothered him. He knew they were safe with Perry in charge.

"Good job on setting up the round lodge and starting a fire. For your reward..." Perry beckoned for Nadia and Lincoln to follow him, and Nadia let out another squeal of excitement. It was time for the hot springs. Lincoln had to admit he was excited, too. After a week of cold baths, the naturally heated waters would be divine.

His anticipation built as they neared their destination. He heard the tell-tale sound of water, but it quickly became apparent that they were not alone. He heard quiet chattering underscored by gurgling geothermal pools. At first, he wondered if the sound of talking was a trick of the mist, but as they drew closer, the voices became more distinct.

Lincoln hesitated. He was not in the mood to be swamped by fans, especially not in his current state. "Is this a tourist spot?" he asked uneasily.

"No," Perry muttered. "No one is usually here. Stay put. I'll go check it out."

Nadia crossed her arms and blew out a breath, stirring her hair. "What do you think this is about?"

"I'm not sure, but it doesn't look like part of Perry's anally retentive plans."

She smiled at the reference to Perry's inflexibility. Lincoln studied her silhouette in the darkness, and she caught him staring. "So, how are you feeling about last night?" she asked quietly. He felt the heat creep over his face and shook his head, smiling shyly.

"I got the impression from Perry that neither one of us should be *feeling* anything."

Nadia giggled. "Maybe I should rephrase the question."

"Yeah," he snorted, chuckling.

Nadia took a step closer. "Did you like it?"

Lincoln looked away and took his time answering. Had he liked it? He had enjoyed every second of it—submitting to passion, exploring his sexual fantasies. There was no way to explain how gratifying it had been. "Best sex I ever had. I've got *almost* no regrets. Was it good for you?" He met Nadia's gaze, and she fondled the collar of his shirt.

Her seductive smile lured him to her mouth, and he gently bussed her lips. Her soft laughter turned into a moan, and she leaned into his arms. "I don't think I'm a greedy woman, but I could get used to this. No strings attached."

Lincoln read the bittersweet awareness in her eyes that there would be no getting used to anything as far as the three of them was concerned. Their adventure was a fleeting one that would be over soon. Before Lincoln could respond, Perry returned with a scowl, prompting the two of them to step away from each other.

"Let's go," Perry said gruffly.

"What's going on?" Lincoln asked.

"Rick Feldman," he spat. "We had an agreement. He would stick to his side of the mountain, and I would stick to mine. Now, suddenly, he's on my turf, and I want answers. Come on. He's meeting me back at our camp in ten minutes."

"So, no hot springs?" Nadia threw up her hands in disbelief.

"I'm sorry, guys. We'll have our chance to soak in the springs tomorrow sometime. Let's go."

They trudged back to the camp to wait for the Empowered Survival instructor. The trio was on guard when Rick Feldman stepped into the circle of light from the campfire a few minutes later. Lincoln eyed the new arrival with barely concealed contempt. Lincoln refrained from analyzing why Perry inspired such a protective, defensive stance. He just knew Rick Feldman had sleaze ball written all over him, and he hated to see his friends abused.

"Cozy little camp," Rick grinned. "I almost didn't find you."

Perry's shoulders stiffened as he rose to his feet and confronted the other man with arms crossed. "Cut the crap, Rick. Why's *your* group using *my* hot springs?" he asked. Rick spread his hands innocently.

"I had a few students who wondered if we might stumble across Lincoln Easley out here, and I decided to try to give them what they wanted. It was a long shot, Perry. How was I to know for sure you'd be at the springs? I was just humoring them."

"Yeah, well, the same way you have an obligation to your students, I have an obligation to mine. That means protecting their privacy and making sure no one invades their space. This side of the mountain isn't big enough for the both of us."

"Point taken," Rick backed off.

A look of suspicion flitted over Perry's face, but he quickly concealed it. "Thank you," he said warily.

"Not a problem." Rick ambled toward Lincoln and held out a card. "When you get tired of rolling around in the mud with this guy, give me a call. My group stays in a chalet with a fully stocked pantry, fantastic showers and working internet."

"Then, what kind of survival guru does that make you?" Lincoln asked. Rick chuckled and walked off, not bothering to answer.

Lincoln moved to toss the card into the fire.

"Not tempted to keep it?" Perry asked.

"What for?"

"He came all this way for you."

"No, thanks. I already have a survival training instructor. Rick Feldman can scavenge for celebrities elsewhere." Lincoln dropped the business card and watched the flames eat away at the paper until it disintegrated.

"Thank goodness he doesn't know who I am," Nadia sighed. "What are we going to do about this, Perry? I doubt the guy will stay away, and now his group knows where we are. I bet good money they'll come snooping around."

Perry went into his backpack and brought out a set of cowbells. "It's late, and it's dark. We can't do anything about it tonight, but tomorrow we can set up perimeter alarms so if anyone gets too close, we'll hear them."

"And any extracurricular activities will be done in the lodge," Nadia suggested. Perry cut a glance at her, but he did not say anything. Lincoln watched the exchange warily.

No one could know they were sleeping together, and if Rick stuck around, they would have to stop. Lincoln wanted things to end on their terms, not someone else's. But if it was "just sex," why not *just stop*? Perry and Nadia would not fit into his future.

He had worked out his destiny: Once he completed the three-week survival training, he would return to Los Angeles and audition for Mitch Trepan's movie. Then, he would score the role and go on to receive high-acclaim for his portrayal of the protagonist in the man versus nature flick. He was sure he would be cast in the role...Well, mostly sure.

"I need another favor," Lincoln murmured.

Perry grabbed a piece of wood from the pile of kindling and started whittling. The campfire painted him warm umber, and shadows slanted over his handsome face. He looked like something out of an old western. He looked good. "What kind of favor?" Perry asked warily.

"I saw you talking on your phone early this morning."

"Checking in on Clyde. He's been released from the hospital. What about it?"

"I know you don't want us relying on technology, but it was unrealistic of me to think I could do without regular communication with my team. My livelihood depends on it. I need to contact my agent and find out what's going on in LA."

Nadia stepped out of the round lodge and seconded Lincoln. "He's right. I need to call my father, as well."

"You two are determined to change the way I do things," Perry sighed.

"Only where it matters." Lincoln grinned.

~

Perry tossed Lincoln his cellphone and left his students to make their phone calls while he made a perimeter sweep. He was more bothered about Empowered Survival showing up than he had let on to Rick. The odds of someone discovering the trio in a clandestine moment increased exponentially when stalker fans were crashing around the woods.

Perry knew the answer to his problem was to not sleep with Nadia and Lincoln again, but after last night, he could not stay away. Pushing into Lincoln's body had been sheer bliss. Nadia's cries of abandonment still echoed in his ears, and walking away was definitely not an option.

He bristled at the fact Rick had given Lincoln his business card—payback for Perry handing out his own back at the hotel. He knew Rick was only trying to recruit the actor to put him out of business. It did not seem to matter that Empowered Survival was doing fine without sabotaging Survive Anything. Perry sensed that his rival's feelings of inadequacy fueled the competition between them.

When he returned to camp, Nadia was still on the phone, and Lincoln was sketching her portrait. Nadia ended her call and handed her phone back to Perry with a grateful smile as he settled by the fire.

He reached into his pack for some of the rabbit jerky they had made together midweek. It would have to do for the night. With Rick nearby, he was in no mood to forage or track down food, and the savory hickory smoked jerky was a welcome treat. He handed Nadia and Lincoln their portions and nibbled a morsel, taking it down with water from the canteen. "Well, we've got nothing better to do. Let's talk," Perry sighed.

"Have we sunk to the new low of needing to make small talk to get through the night?" Lincoln grumbled.

"Humph! You're lucky we can do that, with Rick Feldman and crew are out there. I don't want to do anything...incriminating...So, what's your upcoming movie about?"

Lincoln lifted his brows and shrugged lethargically, "Mitch Trepan, the director who filmed my last movie, told me this famous screenwriter named Landon Ashville created the role just for me..."

"You don't seem too enthusiastic about it," Perry noted. Lincoln wore a studied frown, and the jovial atmosphere that had been in place before Rick Feldman had paid a visit was now well and truly gone.

Lincoln finally set aside his charcoal and looked at him. "That's because, rumor has it, another actor has been given the part. Here I am, wasting my time at a stupid survival training camp, and Jasper Kent is taking my place in LA."

"That's terrible, Lincoln! I can't believe they did that to you," Nadia empathized.

"It is what it is," Lincoln muttered.

Perry shifted uncomfortably. Would the bad news have any bearing on how the actor judged his course? Perry had been looking forward to the publicity, knowing Lincoln would mention his experience with Survive Anything in behind-the-scenes interviews. It was all Lincoln had talked about during the previous week. Now, he looked as if the wind had left his sails.

Perry tried to cheer him up. "There will be other roles. I know that's not what you want to hear right now, but I think you're forgetting that you're a talented, driven young man. I mean, playwrights are writing roles tailor-made for you..." He trailed off, peering into the underbrush on the outskirts of the camp.

"Yeah," Nadia picked up, "don't let this get you—"

"Shh!" Perry slashed a hand through the air, suddenly on high alert. He squinted at the yellow eyes glowing back at him. He heard the unmistakable snarl of a wolf, and Nadia gasped and turned to him with wide eyes. "Don't turn your back on it!"

"Oh, my God!" she gasped.

"Calm down. Absolutely no need for panic."

"What is it doing?" Lincoln asked as he woodenly turned his head to watch the rangy wolf loping past him. By Perry's count, there were three of four of them, and they moved soundlessly around the camp, looking for a point of weakness. He slowly reached for his weapon as he calculated how much time he had before the beasts pounced on them.

His students looked to him for answers, and he hated to tell them this threat had caught him with his pants down. He had been so consumed with the Rick Feldman situation and Lincoln's unexpected news that he had not given this scenario a thought.

One of the wolves bayed, and an answering howl came from roughly a mile to the east. The haunting sound raised the hair on the back of Perry's neck.

"The pack must have circled around. I heard them hunting in the distance earlier this evening."

"Well, don't just sit there. Kill it!" Nadia squeaked hoarsely.

"The problem with that plan, sweetheart," Perry chuckled, "is there's more than one wolf out there, and there's only one way we're gonna get out of this without getting attacked by the whole pack. On the count of three...One...two...three!"

"Do what?" Lincoln asked desperately.

"Make all the noise you can!"

CHAPTER 10

Perry lurched to his feet and fired his gun three times in the air. The deafening blasts made Nadia jump and scream at the top of her lungs and Lincoln jumped up and waved his arms maniacally. The three of them turned the peaceful, quiet night into a madhouse, but it was not enough.

One of the bolder wolves lunged toward Nadia, and its wicked jaws snapped at her pantleg. "Oh, my God! Perry!" she screamed as the wolf started dragging her.

"Perry, do something!" Lincoln yelled.

"I'm trying!"

His eyes widened and his heart rate skyrocketed as he aimed at the beast. Nadia kicked wildly at the wolf's snout. Perry swore anxiously, afraid a bullet would strike her. And the feral glint in the wolf's eyes indicated zero fear.

"Perry! Help me! Please!" Nadia shrieked. Another wolf moved from the side but skipped away when the pack leader growled threateningly. Perry fired in the air again. Another animal attacked her from the other side and dragged at her jacket.

"No! No!" Perry shouted over her screams of panic. He picked up a stone and threw it at the animal while trying to drag her away. Taking a cue from him, Lincoln scrabbled for stuff to throw. The aggressive wolf thrashed his head from side to side, trying to sink his teeth deeper into Nadia's boot, but one of her kicks connected, and the animal let out a blood curdling yelp.

With her leg free, she whipped her hunting knife out of her boot and slashed at the wolf tugging her jacket. "Get away from me!" she growled. The blade cut through thick fur, and the animal howled.

Perry dove toward her, wrestling a branch from the fire. He waved it threateningly in the wolf's face. The straggler finally raced after his peers, and the underbrush shook as the wolves distanced themselves from the scene.

"Oh, my fucking God!" Nadia exclaimed, shaking.

"Let me see. Let me see!" Perry checked her ankle. The boot was scarred from teeth marks, but the leather was unbroken. He checked her arm and pushed a finger through a jagged tear in the fabric of her sleeve, but her skin was unbroken. Her throat was probably raw, but she was otherwise unharmed. She threw her arms around him and hugged him tightly.

Nadia whispered shakily. "What in the holy fucking hell!"

"Why did they come and how do we keep them away?" Lincoln asked, struggling to keep his voice even.

"Someone must have fed them at some point. Once wolves associate humans with food, they'll approach other humans, looking for more of the same. I've never had wolves this close to my camp, but it's a wake-up call. We should put our cooking fire further away from camp and keep food out of our sleeping area."

"Will that be enough?" Nadia stared into the darkness, her heart still racing from the terrifying encounter. Perry placed a reassuring hand on her shoulder.

"They'll stay away. They were probably just curious. By kicking up such a fuss, we showed them humans are more trouble than they're worth. But, if it makes you more comfortable, I'll stay up and keep watch. Why don't you guys get some sleep? We'll get up early in the morning and try the hot springs again."

"I'll keep watch with you," Lincoln mumbled.

"We can take turns," Nadia offered. "How do you expect me to sleep if I'm in the lodge worried about you two? Wake me up when it's my shift."

She made herself as comfortable as possible on her bough bed. The campfire made the round lodge downright cozy, but Nadia was too ramped up from the encounter with the wolves. Not for the first time, she wondered why she was subjecting herself to this nightmare.

It did not help that her phone call with her father was a reminder of everything she was missing while here in the woods. Wilson Marson was at a fundraising gala in south Florida, chumming it up with other wealthy CEOs and socialites. Nadia closed her eyes and pictured the clothes, the food, the accommodations. She distanced herself from the dark, scary woods, but it was not enough.

With two weeks to go, she was not sure she could keep up her enthusiasm for wilderness living. She understood Lincoln's disillusionment with this whole affair. After all, how much of her own life was passing her by while she played survivalist with her two sexy companions?

As for Perry, he was careful not to make a fuss about hosting an actor and a billionaire as students, but she knew his business would benefit from their patronage. Less so now though, as Lincoln would not be in high demand if he didn't get the part he was in training for.

She wanted to help Perry out too, but she had no idea how. Nadia had chosen Survive Anything precisely because it was underrated. Every other place she called boasted much bigger class sizes. She was sold when she called to inquire about the course and Clyde MacAskill told her Perry averaged two or three students per class.

"Are you asleep?" Lincoln whispered as he slipped into the lodge.

She shook her head drowsily. "Too much on my mind."

"Same here, I'm thinking about going back, Nadia. There's no reason for me to stick this out now."

She held out her slender hand, and after a slight pause, Lincoln took it and moved closer to her. She swept his wavy hair back from his face. "Stick it out for me," she suggested. "Perry and I need you. I'm sure he's banking on an endorsement. I know you don't think you're getting much out of this, but the training might come in handy in the future."

"Get some rest." He kissed her fingertips and wrapped an arm around her, closing his eyes, signaling that he no longer wanted to talk. Nadia sighed and snuggled closer. There was no real way she could help either Lincoln or Perry. Just as they could not help her. It seemed this trip was a placeholder between what they wanted and what they would ultimately get.

Lincoln would likely not get the role and, as a result, Perry would not get the publicity. And she would not get to choose what she did with the rest of her life. Fate had already picked their paths out of the wilderness, and the only thing left to do was cherish what little time they had together.

~

Early the next morning, Lincoln stepped out of the tree line and into a picture postcard. Nestled among lush greenery, a trickling stream made its way down the mountainside to tiered pools of bright blue. Steam rose from the tranquil water, and he concluded that he had never seen anything so inviting.

Perry stood at the edge of the springs with hands on hips and a jaunty grin. "Welcome to the most exciting lesson of your three-week stay," he announced. "This week we'll focus on survival health and wellbeing. People have touted the healing powers of geothermal springs for generations, and your first assignment will be to test out the theory. Does this water feel fantastic, or what?"

"Ooh! Good humor and wit! I like this new you," Nadia laughed. She whipped her shirt over her head and threw her pants aside. Lincoln chuckled and shed his own clothes a little more slowly.

Nadia and Perry seemed both rested and exuberant, despite a third of the night spent keeping watch. Lincoln had not slept well though. He had nightmares of fading into obscurity. He kept hearing Mitch Trepan's voice in his head. *It's a lot of character to carry.* In the end, Mitch would likely choose to go with a less experienced actor, forcing Lincoln to contemplate what that meant. He thought he was past cold calls and waiting patiently in line for his opportunity.

It was doubly disappointing because so much of his true personality was sacrificed to make the man Hollywood demanded of him—assertive, cavalier, unfeeling. A Neanderthal version of himself he suddenly questioned. Not only did he feel the survival training course was in vain, but his whole life was a series of steps further and further away from his true nature.

Fate seemed to be saying, "Not yet," just when he thought his opportunity to show himself worthy was at hand. Landon Ashville's script was more than lots of running around, posing with guns, and minimal dialogue. It was an in-depth look at how the will to survive could shape and mold a man into a better version of himself.

Lincoln eased into the water, and he winced at the unexpected heat. The steamy pool was cooled by surface water, but it was like sinking into a hot tub. When Nadia swam toward him, she managed to make him smile. Her lithe body took his mind off his problems and forced him back into the moment.

"This is unbelievable, Perry," she murmured dreamily.

"Was it worth the wait?" Perry asked. Lincoln tilted his head to the side and watched Nadia flow into Perry's arms.

"It reminds me of why I don't want to take the job my father has for me back home."

"What's the job?" Lincoln asked.

"He wants me to work in one of our labs, but we don't see eye to eye on environmental concerns," she said with a shrug. "Now, it seems he's worn me down. When I leave from here, I belong to big oil. I become a part of the problem, whether I want to or not."

"Why don't you stand up to him?"

"I've tried! But, Dad's right. If I don't do my part, someone else will. At least if I manage to get into the company, I may be able to do some good from the inside." Nadia did not sound convinced by her own line of reasoning, and Lincoln shook his head.

"You struck me as stronger than that," he said.

"Don't add to the pressure. Sounds like she's got enough on her plate," said Perry.

"Hey, I'm just pointing out that, if she truly doesn't want to be a part of the problem, she'll walk away from the job offer, join Greenpeace or something. Sounds to me like she's taking the line of least resistance. I can't imagine anyone being in a beautiful place like this and then shrugging off our obligation to protect our environment."

"Don't pretend you have me all figured out, Lincoln Easley," Nadia said. "The only reason you came here was to get a part in a movie. You can't even enjoy this experience because you're too busy feeling sorry for yourself because you have some unexpected competition."

"At least I'm making my own decisions about what to do with my future."

"Oh, that's low, Lincoln! Even for a self-absorbed Hollywood prick like—"

"Hey, hey, hey," Perry interrupted the heated exchange. "We're supposed to be relaxing. Look, I get it. Lincoln, you're upset about not being cast in the role you wanted; and, Nadia, you're at odds with your dad about a job you don't want. But we're still stuck together for the next couple of weeks. So, I suggest you guys take a break from your problems."

"You know what. I can't do that. I've done that enough, and that's what got me into this situation. Had I been home, I may have been able to talk some sense into Mitch about not hiring Jasper Kent."

"Where are you going?"

Lincoln ignored Perry's question and snatched up his clothes, quickly dressing to ward off the cold. "I can find my own way back to the cabin, thanks. I'm sure there's a Lyft or Uber driver willing to make this trip for the right dollar amount." Before Perry could stop him, he set off for camp to pack his belongings. His companions made no effort to follow him.

When he arrived at the round lodge, Lincoln stared back the way he had come. He wished that one or both of his companions would show up. Apparently they were unconcerned that he may get attacked by wolves or could fall off a cliff. Grumbling bitterly, Lincoln rummaged through Perry's pack and found the survival instructor's emergency cellphone.

He grabbed his sketchbook, and it fell open on one of his favorite pictures. He had drawn Perry whittling something while Nadia sat at his knee. Not only did it show his modest artistic skills, it captured a memory he was loathe to leave behind.

But he had dallied in the woods long enough. Sticking around to continue the charade was not worth the risks to his career. He turned north and hiked down the mountain in search of civilization, wondering if Nadia's sweet plea for him to stay last night had been sincere. *Apparently not.* She had not tried to stop him from leaving this time. And that was okay. He was used to pretenders.

~

"Aren't you going after him?" Nadia asked.

"He's not going anywhere. He just needs to let off steam. He'll be waiting at camp when we get there. Besides, don't tell me you're worried about him. You're the one who ran him off."

"I didn't run him off, but nobody talks to me like that. And maybe if you had let on how much you need him, he would have stuck around."

Perry chuckled in amusement. "What the hell are you talking about? How much I need him?"

"I'm not daft, Perry. You forget, I'm a businesswoman. When you found out Lincoln was an actor and I was an heiress, you knew you hit the client jackpot. Just one peachy review from either one of us would put Survive Anything on the map. Unfortunately, your radical self-reliance philosophy means that needing another human being represents failure."

"Well, since we're being candid, Lincoln was right," Perry rejoined. "You'd do well to stand up to your dad and tell him how you really feel, even if you risk disappointing him. If you really don't want the job, you should tell him."

"How can you take Lincoln's side over mine? You're the one who told me to challenge myself, and that's what I'm doing. I'm challenging myself to take on the biggest career break of my life and make it work for me!"

"No, you're bowing out and letting someone else build the fire. And, I'm not taking Lincoln's side. He has his flaws, too. Hell, he's so lost in character that he wouldn't recognize himself in the mirror, but that's neither here nor there."

"I'm not afraid to tell people I need them, I just don't need others. My business was limping along just fine without your endorsements, and I'll continue to run Survive Anything without you two," he fumed, suddenly upset.

"Oh, thank you!" she yelled. "Thank you for permission to ditch your miserable, sadomasochistic survival course. Lincoln had the right idea. I can think of a hundred things I'd rather do than spend two more weeks with you. If he's waiting back at camp, I'll be more than happy to join him getting the hell out of here!"

She launched to her feet, splashed out of the pool and lurched toward her clothes. Perry did not move as he watched her get dressed. "Fine! You can both sit at camp in time-out like misbehaving toddlers. I intend to enjoy the goddamned hot springs."

Perry had spent half the night dreaming up ways he could make the morning special, but Nadia and Lincoln had ruined it with their self-indulgent antics. He could not believe Nadia thought Lincoln had stormed off because he had not given some sentimental speech about needing him. He felt that they were abandoning ship because they both lacked the fortitude to finish the training course, and that was their problem, not his.

He sank deeper in the pool and let the steamy mineral water swirl around him. But the surrounding peace felt more like a silent accusation.

Perry growled in frustration and got out of the hot springs. "I should seriously charge more for the headache of putting up with these two," he complained to nobody in particular. He shrugged into his shirt and pulled on his pants. He thought of alternative, way more pleasant, ways the morning could have ended.

"Nadia, get back here!" he shouted. He trudged through the shrubs and found the familiar path to the clearing he always used for the second-week base camp. Ignoring thorns that snagged at his fatigues, he crashed through the underbrush. Within minutes, he came upon the round lodge, expecting to see Nadia and Lincoln's sheepish faces.

"Nadia? Lincoln?" Perry spun around. They were nowhere in sight. His heart rate rapidly accelerated as he realized he had placed the wrong bet. He rushed into the lodge where he discovered both had taken their belongings with them. Neither had taken any food.

The meager training he had given them probably increased their confidence in their ability to survive alone, but it was a false confidence. Any number of things could go wrong without Perry there to keep them safe. Worse, Clyde was not home to radio for help.

Shaking his head in disbelief, Perry dove on his pack and felt around for his cellphone to call up a search party, but someone had beat him to it. "No, no, no!" he whispered in horror. "Nadia! Lincoln! Get back here! It's not safe!"

He ran to the edge of the clearing and paused to see if he could hear them. He quickly dealt with the fire, covering it with dirt to make sure it was out completely. Then, he snatched up his pack and searched for signs of the direction or directions they had taken.

He swore in despair. He prayed to God he found them both before it was too late.

CHAPTER 11

Nadia stared at the base of the tree, trying to figure out the pattern of moss crawling up its trunk. She remembered that moss always grew on the north side of a tree. Unfortunately, the past few trees she had come upon had not gotten the memo. The pale green plants grew all around the tree trunks.

She gnawed on her bottom lip and took off walking again. Nadia convinced herself the route looked familiar, and she kept up a running pep talk in her head. *I'm not lost. I'm a Marson. I'm rising to the occasion.* She desperately wanted to be right. It had taken the three of them half a day to arrive at the second-week basecamp. If she wanted to make it back to Clyde's cabin before nightfall, she could not afford to get lost.

Nadia stumbled through the underbrush in search of the right pathway. When thorns cut into the exposed skin of her wrists and hands, she ignored the sting. She swatted at gnats and bugs, wondering why they were still so prevalent in late autumn.

"Damn it!" she swore as she killed another mosquito. "This isn't going according to plan. Where the hell is Lincoln? And why hasn't Perry come looking for me, yet?" She knew the answer to that one. She had pushed him away the same way she had pushed Lincoln away.

Nadia hated to think she was the bad guy, but, in this case, she probably was.

A chilly droplet of perspiration rolled down her spine, and she squirmed. Then, she felt another. And another. Nadia realized it was not sweat, but rain. She stared up at the grey sky with dreary resolve. *So be it*, she thought.

She pulled her hunting knife from its sheath and assembled a lean-to for shelter. If she sat still, maybe Perry would stumble upon her. She did not want to crash around through the woods in the rain. Nadia huddled in her makeshift hut and waited for the bad weather to pass over. She thought about the disagreement she had had with each of them back at the hot springs.

Lincoln and Perry had only said what she refused to say to herself. The notebook full of letters to Maria all said the same thing. She wanted to rebel. She wanted to tell her father that he was ruining her life by attempting to take away her autonomy. Wilson Marson made her feel weak and inadequate, even when meaning to empower her.

Her entire life had been about making her father proud. Whether that meant being a goody-two-shoes teacher's pet in high school or studying her way through what was supposed to be her wild college years. At every point, she had put what her father wanted ahead of her own needs.

Nadia wondered if she was afraid to pursue anything serious with Lincoln or Perry because she knew that her father would insert himself into her romantic life, as he had with everything else. At what point would she stand up for herself, if not now? When he was picking her wedding dress and arranging her marriage?

She sighed and crossed her arms to insulate herself as best she could. The rain, was now coming down in thick sheets. She was also getting hungry.

"Alright, Mr. Man Upstairs. Are we back to the bargaining table?" she whispered. She wanted to be back at camp. She wanted Perry to find her so she could apologize for flying off the handle. She wanted Lincoln to come back, as well. The three of them belonged together.

At least for the next two weeks. She sucked in a deep breath. "Perry! Perry, if you can hear me, I'm over here!"

She closed her eyes and rested her head on her folded arms, thinking shouting was useless. The rain nearly drowned out the sound, and Perry was probably warm and cozy in the round lodge, letting them brave the wilds to their hearts' content. A tear beaded at the corner of her eye. The wind picked up as the raindrops turned to icy slush. She scooted away from a puddle that threatened to spill into her lean-to.

"Perry, I'm sorry," she said quietly. "I'm cold, and I'm scared. I made a mistake. Please, find me."

"Nadia!" The voice was faint and far off, but it was very real. Nadia sat up excitedly.

"Perry? Perry! Over here!" she shrieked.

"Keep talking to me! Nadia, I'm coming!"

"This way! Oh, my God! I'm so glad you heard me! Perry!"

Suddenly, he sprinted through the threes. Nadia had never been so happy to see a wild man in the woods in her life. She launched into his arms, and he hugged her tightly. Both laughed with relief as the rain fell around them. He cupped her face and kissed her hard.

"What in the hell were you trying to prove? Were you trying to kill me with worry?" he whispered against her lips. She giggled and nuzzled closer, raising a brow at the fact he had worried about her.

"I didn't think it would be this bad," she admitted. "I thought I would run into Lincoln."

"You went west, Nadia. He went north. You're not even going down the mountain. You're climbing."

"Oh, my gosh!"

"'Oh, my gosh' is right. Come on. Let me get you back to camp and get you warm and dry. Then, I have to go back out and find Lincoln."

"You mean, you haven't found him yet?"

Perry shook his head glumly. "Let's hope he accidentally circled back like you did. You're only about fifteen minutes from where you started. If he didn't, I guess I can kiss that good review goodbye, right?"

≈

L incoln shielded his head with his extra shirt, but cold rain battered him anyway. As he jogged through the storm, mud puddles soaked through his sturdy combat boots, making the trip almost unbearable. But, according to the compass on Perry's cellphone, he was going in the right direction. He would be back at Clyde's cabin in a few hours.

Just in case he was off the mark, Lincoln tore another drawing from his sketchbook. The sheet of paper fluttered out of his hand, and the slushy rain dampened it and anchored it to the ground. He still worried the gusty wind would carry it off any second. Lincoln squinted behind him and saw similar sheets littering the path he had taken. If Perry found it within himself to come looking for him, the paper trail would help.

And, if not, Lincoln had to find his own way. He pressed the cellphone between his cheek and his shoulder and tried to talk over the thunderous downpour when his call connected. "Hello? Hello, this is Lincoln Easley! I'm looking for my agent, Dominic. Is he there?"

"I'm sorry. He's out of the office," said the woman who answered. "Lincoln? It's Carmen! Remember me?"

Carmen, Carmen...He rolled the name around in his head until he put a face to the name. While trying to puzzle it out, he stepped into a hole and sank to the shin in ice cold water. He yelped involuntarily, but the bracing shock did the trick, and he remembered her. "Carmen, from *Vengeance with a Vengeance*? Hi! What are you doing in Dominic's office?"

"It's kind of embarrassing. He needed a new personal assistant, and my dad thought I needed the—Lincoln? I can hardly hear myself over the noise in the background. What *is* that? Are you there?"

"Yes, don't hang up! I'm sorry for the noise. I'm just—I'm stuck outside in a rainstorm. Who should be more embarrassed?" He tried to laugh.

"Oh, my goodness! Are you okay?"

"Well, I hate to be pessimistic, but I think I might be lost. Hopefully, I'm not too far off the beaten path." *Why am I making small talk at a time like this?* Lincoln squinted up at the relentless deluge, unsure how much more rain he could take. He dropped the charming self-deprecation and got straight to the point. "Listen, I need Dominic to call me back at this number as soon as possible. It's an emergency. Tell him have a car sent out to get me to the airport."

"A car? Let's see," Carmen hummed speculatively and rustled papers around. Lincoln bit his inner cheek to keep from losing patience. There should have been nothing to 'let's see' about. He needed a car. Pronto. "No, Dominic didn't leave any instructions about sending a car for you. I'm looking at your schedule right here, and he has you down for a survival training course for another two weeks."

"Yes, I know, but there's been a change of plans. I'm not staying— Ow! Shit!" He yowled as he stepped in another hidden pitfall. His ankle rolled beneath him, sending shards of pain shooting up his leg. Agony took him to the soggy ground where he sat and stared at his throbbing lower extremity with a grimace.

"Are-Are you okay?"

"Please stop asking me that. Carmen, get in touch with Dominic. I don't care how you get it done. I just need you to get me connected to him."

"I can't! He's out of reach for the next few days. Holiday with one of his girlfriends. And I've only been working here for a week. I don't know how—Wait, just give me an address. I'll put a car on the company account. Hopefully, he won't mind."

Lincoln's spirits sank even further. "I don't have the address; Dominic has it."

"I feel terrible about this, Lincoln. I want to help. Should I call nine-one-one? You said it was an emergency."

"No! No, don't do that. My instructor is somewhere around here. I guess I'll have to go back," he sighed. "Me and my goddamned ego! I got upset about something he said, and I stormed off, but I don't think the situation is dire. At least, not yet."

"I hope you're not putting on a brave face for my account. I need to know for certain that when I hang up this phone, I'm not signing your death warrant."

Lincoln chuckled. "You have my word. When I end this call, I'm turning right around and finding Perry."

"And, if you don't find him, you'll call me back, right?"

"Absolutely, Carmen. Good luck with your acting, by the way. Don't let a little setback keep you down."

"Oh, it's not what you think! My dad is Herschel Wilde. You know, the reality TV producer? I can get back in front of a camera anytime, but he seems to think holding down a day job builds character. And, anyway, he's friends with Dominic, so..."

"Got it. Well, I better get going. Tell Dom to call me when he can." He smiled and ended the call, coming back to reality. He had channeled confidence into the phone call, but it was the false kind. He was still on the ground in the rain with a rolled ankle. "Take your own advice, Lincoln. Don't let a little setback keep you—" He tried to rise, but his foot would not support his weight. "Down," he groaned.

He scooted to the nearest tree and drew his wet shirt around him, shivering and miserable. But he knew he could not wait for the storm to pass. Not if he intended to return to Perry and Nadia near the hot springs. Lincoln painstakingly ripped his saturated shirt into strips of fabric and hobbled over to a broken tree branch. Using sticks to splint his foot, he padded it with what was left of the tattered shirt and used the strips to bind it in place.

Then, he grabbed his hunting knife and cut a branch to use as a walking stick. With his makeshift crutch in place, Lincoln consulted the compass on Perry's phone and turned south. He was grateful that the ascent was easy. He was cold, wet and hungry, and it was getting late.

During the grueling trek, Lincoln had no choice but to examine himself and figure out how he had gotten into this mess. He wanted to blame it on Nadia and Perry for goading him into leaving the safety of camp, but it was not their fault. Nadia correctly assessed his reasons for being on the trip—self-serving reasons that had everything to do with his own oversized ego and with cultivating his image in Hollywood.

Like the character in Landon Ashville's screenplay—a character written expressly for Lincoln—he should have faced the wilderness and come out a better man. Instead, he had undergone the training solely for his career. When his ego and self-righteousness had been checked, Lincoln had thrown his toys and stormed off like a petulant child.

Lincoln sneezed and sniffed, hoping he was not catching a cold. He had miles left to go in an uncertain direction. He wanted to show Nadia and Perry he was ready to drop the act. He might have been there to prepare for a role before, but now he was going back to find himself.

CHAPTER 12

Rolling thunder rumbled through the forest. "Give me a break, will you?" Perry growled at the sky as he ran. The rain had eased off, but the continuing cold drizzle made the journey tough. His heart was ready to burst, and his panted breaths wheezed from his chest. He ignored the strain. This was life or death. He had to find Lincoln.

A potent sense of déjà vu assailed him. He was back on the battle-field. The mission had gone wrong. His best friend had been taken by enemy forces. The same heart-rending despair clouded his senses this time—with Lincoln captive to only the fickle elements and his own underappreciation for what nature could do—but Perry prayed for a better ending to this story, because he could not bear to lose someone else he cared about.

Lincoln had asked him why he left the military and he'd used his injury as an excuse. Truth be told, it was this one failed mission that destroyed him. The scar tissue that burned under his shoulder blade from where hot shrapnel had done its worst was of no real conse-quence. The mental scar from failing to save his friend was a different matter entirely, that one would never heal.

Perry had been honorably discharged. The official reason was

PTSD. Unofficially, depression and grief had rendered him incapable of doing his job. He had returned to civilian life, determined to keep people out, never wanting to experience loss again. But somehow Nadia and Lincoln had gotten under his skin and into his soul. If he lost them, he did not know what he would do.

His eyes zoomed in on a fluttering piece of paper whipped along by the wind, and he slowed his mad dash to examine it. As he snatched it from the tree branch it was hooked upon, his hands trembled. It was one of Lincoln's sketches.

"I'm on the right track," he whispered. "Lincoln!" he shouted. His booming voice echoed for miles. He had to be close, but he had no idea which way to go. "Lincoln, goddamn it! Where are you?"

Perry heard a sneeze and sniffle somewhere up ahead. Then, he heard his name called out weakly. He dropped the sketch and sprinted in the direction of the sound. Something was wrong. He sensed it. His mind conjured a million bad endings. Anything could have happened to Lincoln in the hours they had been separated. He forced his legs to keep pumping.

When he finally saw him, his heart dropped. "Lincoln," he gasped. His haggard-looking student and lover huddled in the freezing cold rain with a rough cast encircling his lower leg.

"I knew you would find me." Lincoln smiled wanly as he slumped against a nearby fallen log to rest.

Perry kneeled before him, gingerly running his fingers along his injured leg. "What happened?"

"I think I twisted my ankle. Mmph!" Lincoln grimaced and bit back a whimper as Perry ran his ankle through a range of motion.

"I'm sorry to hurt you, but I have to check. It's not broken. Looks like a bad sprain." Perry swore softly at the dilemma. The ankle was tender and swollen and walking on it had to be excruciating. Lincoln sneezed several times in a row, and Perry stroked his forehead to check for fever. "We've gotta get you out of the rain."

"I can't make it," Lincoln moaned, shaking his head.

"Yes, you can. You're just hungry and tired. Here, eat this."

Praying he was right, Perry rummaged through his pack and found the last of the jerky. He pressed some to Lincoln's lips as he uncorked the canteen, urging him to drink. Some of the color returned to Lincoln's face, and Perry breathed a quiet sigh of relief.

"Fuck, it's c-cold," Lincoln stuttered, trying to laugh it off. A surge of affection poured through Perry as he stroked his face again.

"I know. I know."

Perry decided protection from the rain was the first order of business. Working against the clock, he quickly constructed a sturdy lean-to with evergreen branches, piling on the pine needles until all but the most determined raindrops were kept out.

Emergency supplies were in his pack to build a fire. He used his hatchet to split and shave a branch for dry wood and kindling. The simple act seemed to take forever, and he glared up at the darkening sky. He had to move faster to keep Lincoln from falling victim to hypothermia. Perry pulled some accelerant-soaked cotton balls out of a Ziploc bag and nestled a few between the slats of his hastily built bridge of sticks. Then, he ignited the assemblage.

"You asshole," Lincoln tried to laugh. "You m-made us build a fire from scratch."

"Desperate times call for desperate measures. You need heat. Let's get you out of those wet clothes," he whispered. The fire burned brighter as Perry ripped off Lincoln's shirt and shed his own. He dragged him against his bare chest, imparting body heat, as he pressed his nose to Lincoln's neck and inhaled gratefully. Perry dropped a soft kiss on his shoulder and hugged him tighter. "Better? How's the ankle?"

"It only hurts when there's weight on it," Lincoln breathed. "The pants are wet, too." Chuckling, Perry brought a dry shirt from his pack and wrapped it around Lincoln's upper body. He got him out of his pants, taking care not to hurt his ankle as he wrestled them off.

Perry drew an emergency thermal blanket from his pack and cloaked them both. He sat against the log, sheltered by the lean-to, with Lincoln in his arms. He rocked him until his tremors ceased. The rain slacked off. The temperature dropped another few degrees.

Perry squared his jaw, ignoring his desire. Lincoln was flush against his body. He absently ran a hand up and down the actor's torso. When his fingers skimmed lower, Lincoln moaned softly and moved toward his touch. Perry's fingertips grazed his manhood. He licked his lips, contemplating taking things further. They had to get back to camp, but his body was screaming for sex.

He kissed the back of Lincoln's neck and listened to him sigh in pleasure. Perry tenderly stroked his cock. He was warm and hard in his palm, and his veins pulsated with his racing heart rate. Desire radiated off him in waves. Perry could not resist the temptation.

Memories of the first time Lincoln had touched him came to mind. The first time they had sex. He kissed Lincoln's shoulder and gripped him tighter. Parting his lips, he licked a silky trail up the side of his neck and found Lincoln's mouth seeking his. He whimpered as Perry's tongue swept deeper. Tension coiled around them both—a tangible ache that begged for release.

As Perry masturbated him with increasing eagerness, Lincoln kissed him harder, thrusting into his hand. The glide of his cock in and out of Perry's grip made his loins tighten expectantly, and he pulled Lincoln into his lap. "I want to be inside of you," he whispered. Lincoln nodded. "But we have to be quick. I can't keep you out—"

Lincoln quickly nodded again and shushed him. "Just do it..."

Perry closed his eyes and reached between them to free his erection. He soaked his manhood with spit and eased into the crease, guiding Lincoln down his shaft. They both breathed faster as he navigated deeper. Perry tried to take his time, but the quiet sound of Lincoln's encouraging moans made him want to ram harder. "Oh, yes," he groaned. "Faster..."

As Lincoln rose and fell on his cock, the tantalizing draw of his asshole sucked Perry deeper and released him with agonizing slowness. He hooked his arms under Lincoln's and gripped his shoulders for leverage. Thrusting up and into him, Perry took control.

His face contorted in a grimace of bliss as their bodies slammed together. The wet, sexy sound of ecstasy echoed in the deepening twilight. Perry had lost track of time. He splayed a hand over Lincoln's chest. Lincoln gasped his name and shuddered. "Perry!"

"Yes! Uhn! Fuck," he grunted.

He could not get enough of him. He pressed Lincoln to the ground and mounted him from behind.

"Are you sure you're up for this?"

Lincoln nodded, swamped with desire. "Yes."

"Yes, sir," Perry corrected him. Lincoln giggled quietly as Perry nuzzled the side of his face and pushed deeper. His silent hiss of pleasure feathered over Lincoln's neck and stirred a wanton moan in response. Perry rapidly escalated the already intense sex. "Just forgive me in advance."

"For what?" Lincoln gasped, rocking to meet Perry's passionate thrusts. Perry clasped his chin and dove a finger into his mouth, and Lincoln eagerly sucked. Perry swore as he bucked harder.

"I might not last," he growled as he nibbled his earlobe. "I've been daydreaming about doing this all night. I can't get you out of my head. I can't get either of you out of my goddamned head!"

At the confession, Lincoln writhed with excitement. The air was thick with ozone from the storm. The loamy smell of earth rose from the damp grass near his face, adding to the primal lust that cut through him. Lincoln was acutely aware of how dire the situation had been a half hour ago when Perry found him. Now that he was safe with Perry, the danger seemed a lifetime away.

Every stroke set nerve endings afire. He was filled to the brim with pleasure. Perry pressed a hand to the base of his spine and fucked him harder. His moist lips skimmed Lincoln's neck and shoulders in hot, seductive kisses that made him whine for more. They grinded together as one, straining to reach the pinnacle.

Perry doused Lincoln's crease with more spit, and his thick, hard shaft penetrated and touched his very soul. Lincoln emitted a strangled moan as he clenched the grass beneath his hand. There was no way to pretend he was not affected. He fluidly rocked his pelvis to swallow and release him. He heard their slick connection. He reveled in Perry's responses. The chorus of their pleasure climbed to crescendo in loud outcries and ragged exhales.

"God, you're huge," Lincoln groaned.

"You want me to stop?"

"Hell, no!"

Lincoln's body stretched to accommodate his lover. Perry was balls-deep in his ass, and Lincoln was shocked at how good it felt to surrender. The first time at the hotel, he had been nervous, worried about what it meant that he wanted this man. The second time at camp, he had been open to the experience but unsure what to expect. This encounter was different. This time he knew what he wanted, and he chased the thrill with abandon.

Perry sobbed his name and jerked his head back by a fistful of hair. Lincoln hungrily kissed him, gasping. His ears reddened with exertion. He had entirely forgotten the throbbing pain in his ankle. Perry clasped his hip and rocked faster in and out of his tight sheath. His dewy pre-cum lubricated his passage as he prodded Lincoln's prostate and begged him to let go. A riotous blossom of ecstasy unfurled in Lincoln's core, and he shifted on his side to masturbate.

His erection hardened in his hand. The head of his cock glistened as he circled around with his palm and brought his fingers back down to his balls. He squeezed and massaged himself in tandem to Perry's expert stroke. All the years Lincoln had wondered what it would be like to be with someone like the buff, muscular survivalist. His fantasies had never even come close to the reality.

His pelvis jerked involuntarily, and Lincoln gritted his teeth. Another wave of ecstasy washed over him. His mouth dropped open in a silent scream. His body levitated, anchored only by Perry's arm across his chest. He rocked harder, taking his cock faster and deeper. It was unbelievably freeing.

"Fuck me! Ah, Perry!"

"Uhn! You're so fucking amazing," Perry grunted. "Tell me your sexy ass is mine."

"It is! Ah, yes!"

Fireworks went off behind Lincoln's closed eyes as he whimpered. Groaning, Perry lifted Lincoln's leg and angled deeper. He captured his mouth in another fiery kiss, and Lincoln melted against his warm chest. He surrendered everything, taking the punishing strokes that made his libido surge. The impromptu sex was quickly becoming the best he had ever had.

"Now, tell me again, it's mine," Perry whispered.

"It's yours," Lincoln gasped. At the soft-spoken command, he thought he would explode. His abs clenched in anticipation as Perry rammed him with increasing fervor. His hand blurred, stroking his pounding cock. He dripped with excitement. He inhaled sharply, moaning. "It's...yours!"

His steel pipe blasted jizz all over his stomach and chest. Lincoln cried out in bliss as spasms jerked his erection higher and more of his spunk cascaded down his thick, throbbing shaft. The sight of it seemed to drive Perry over the edge. He swept a hand over Lincoln's rippling abs, touching the silky liquid. He ran it down Lincoln's dick and squeezed the last drops free. Grunting, he suddenly pulled out.

"Where do you want it?" Perry asked desperately.

Lincoln opened his mouth. Perry rose on his knees near his face. He clutched the crown of his head with one hand and his own quaking erection with the other, and he jerked off against Lincoln's lips. Within seconds, Perry threw his head back and growled fiercely as he climaxed, painting Lincoln's face in a shower of pearly cum.

Lincoln moaned hungrily as he licked away Perry's nectar. His body tingled with desire, and his heart raced at the taboo act, but he wanted it. He sucked Perry's erupting cock into his mouth and rolled his tongue over his warm hardness. Sighing in pleasure, he finally released him and fell back to stare up at the beautiful man who had saved his life.

~

"When I said we were learning health and well-being this week," Perry murmured, "I didn't mean I wanted you to get sick so I could nurse you back to health." Nadia carefully brought a cup of warm ginger tea to Lincoln's lips and urged him to sip.

"What happened?" Lincoln coughed.

"After I found you and brought you back, you were so exhausted, you damn near passed out," he explained. "You inspired Nadia to run off, too. I couldn't believe the two of you would do something that foolhardy. By the way, you're lucky I didn't cart you to town and charge you with theft for taking my cellphone."

Lincoln grimaced and looked at him with meek, emerald eyes. "I'm sorry."

"He's joking," Nadia chuckled, swatting at Perry.

The instructor softened. "How are you feeling? You've been asleep all night and most of the day. Are you warm enough? Ready to eat?"

"God, yes! I'm so hungry, I could eat a damn moose." Lincoln reached for the bowl Nadia extended to him, but he was struck by another brief coughing spell.

"Baby steps. See if you can get down this stew first. Then, we'll work on a moose." As Perry helped him sit up and spooned a few mouthfuls into him, Nadia hugged herself, scooting closer. "I was worried about you," she whispered.

"We both were," Perry added. "There's something I need to tell you both. I got out of the military because I lost a close friend and went through severe clinical depression. I isolated myself from people because it was easier to do that than to open up and risk loss again. That approach worked for me for years."

"The night at the hotel bar, even before we slept together, the two of you made me remember what I was missing. When we got out here, a part of me wished we could continue that good vibe. The other part wanted to continue with business as usual. I tried hard to keep the boundaries in place, but the second I realized you guys were missing, I knew that I wanted to keep you around."

Nadia smiled teasingly and raked her fingers through his hair. "Are you saying what I think you're saying?"

"I'm saying I like having you two around. I've never been needy," Perry said with a grin, "and you'll never get me to say I need anybody, but I *want* you two here for as long as I can have you. So, what do you say? Can you put up with me for another two weeks?" He spread his hands and Nadia tossed her hair, laughing softly, as she floated into his arms.

"If the alternative is another trek through ice rain, I think I can live with you," she giggled. "I mean, maybe I *am* a bit spoiled, but that just means I know a good thing when I see it. It was crazy to consider giving up on this course when all I've wanted to do for months is learn survival skills. I can't think of a better team to go through this journey with, so I'm in."

Lincoln picked up the bowl of rabbit stew and gestured with the spoon. "Okay, can I be candid? Up to now, this hasn't been my idea of a good time, but I'm willing to try again. I want to be able to get something out of this, something authentic. I tend to become whoever I need to be in any given situation, but out here, with you two, I want to be able to be myself."

Perry stretched, nodding in agreement with Lincoln's self-assessment. "Well, I've been up all night, and my shoulder is killing me from dragging your decidedly attractive ass on a stretcher for miles. I think I deserve a dip in the hot springs. This time without the dramatic blow-up. Anyone else care to join me?"

Lincoln pointed to his ankle. "I don't think I can get there on this without my walking stick."

"You're in luck. I have it right here," Nadia smiled. They had made it through their first bona fide survivor moment and the endorphins and hormones were raging.

CHAPTER 13

They had sex in the hot springs. Nadia relived the moment later that night when she returned to indulge in the natural bath. She left Lincoln and Perry back at camp, and she folded her toiletries in her extra shirt. When she arrived at the serene pools, she wedged her torch between two rocks.

She unbraided her thick, dark hair and sank beneath the rippling water. Her hair floated around her pale face, and she opened her eyes. The water was the clearest blue—so clear that she could see the flame of her torch dancing on the surface. Her body ached in all the right places and all the right ways, and she remembered Lincoln's masterful thrusts, Perry's sensual kisses.

They had held her against the edge of the pool, taking turns ravishing her. When she was weak with desire to come, they had drawn out the torment, edging her until she begged for it. She remembered Perry's rigid staff gliding past her lips and depositing his tangy, salty essence on her tongue. Lincoln had drenched her in his silver rain.

And after that, they did it all over again.

Nadia reemerged from the hot spring with a satisfied sigh, reaching for the soap plant bulb Perry helped her find earlier. She worked the slippery bulb in her hands until it began to lather. Then, wriggling her fingers through her hair, she massaged her scalp. It felt and smelled divine. She wondered if she was finally getting used to the doomsday prepper lifestyle.

She had written to Maria to tell her about getting lost in the woods, knowing her friend would find the story hilarious. But the letter had only served to make Nadia return to the question of what she would do with her feelings when it was time to leave.

Even as she told herself to be sensible, she dreamed up ways to make the polyamorous relationship work. She was moneyed. She could travel. Maybe buy a big house in the woods where Perry would feel comfortable living. Lincoln could work in LA and return home between movies.

She could *not* turn down the job in Texas, however, no matter how much she wanted to—and that was the monkey wrench in her plans. There was no way to keep a healthy relationship going if ninety-five percent of her time was spent in a lab a thousand miles away. Plus, her father would make her life miserable the minute he learned she was dating two men. Of that there was no doubt.

She was a Marson. She was supposed to be modest and conservative. This kind of behavior was unacceptable in her social circle. Nadia lost her train of thought when she heard tinkling bells nearby. It was Perry's alarm system. She hastily swam to the edge of the pool to cover herself, but it was only Lincoln hobbling along the path.

"There I was," he narrated dramatically, "lost in the thick of the woods, pummeled by icy rain, dragging my bum leg. When the last of my strength failed me, the only thing that sustained me was the memory of your glorious face. I owe you half my life, dear lady."

"Only half your life?"

"The other half is indebted to the gallant knight who carried me home."

"I thought you were one of Rick Feldman's minions," she giggled.

"Your instincts are spot-on. He just showed up in camp. I left Perry talking to him. I can't stand to be in the same place with the snake.

Thought you might like some company." He settled on a large stone near the glistening pool and smiled warmly.

Nadia lifted a brow in surprise at his comment. "Perry and Rick are meeting up, what's that about I wonder?"

"From what I heard, Rick is trying to weasel his way into a deal with Perry to blend our groups, but Perry's not having it. I'm sure Rick wants the acclaim he thinks he'll get from having me in his class. If he only knew. I likely don't have anything in the pipeline for months. And, when I do get busy again, I only plan to put Survive Anything on the map. Rick doesn't deserve any good publicity."

"I'm sorry about Jasper Kent," Nadia said softly. Lincoln gave her a small smile. "Don't give up hope. You said that role was written for you, and I believe it. I'll be rooting for you down in Texas."

"Ever thought about moving out west? You could put your degree to use doing something you really like."

"My doctorate," she murmured, looking down. "And, don't talk like that. We all know we don't belong together."

"Yeah, but, what if?" Lincoln pressed. She met his intense blue eyes and saw the questions lurking just below the surface, questions that mirrored her own. *What if they could make it work?* She swallowed thickly and swam to the other side of the pool.

"The problem with our situation is that there are too many of us with too many different goals. That's why we can't be together. You're at the top of your career—"

"Gosh, I hope not," he laughed.

"—And I'm at the start of mine. Perry is comfortable with his solitude. As good as this feels, it's temporary. So, no talk about moving out west, understand?"

He held up his hands in surrender with a playful smile still in place. "Point taken. Would you like me to rinse your hair?"

She presented her back to him, and Lincoln tenderly dunked her silky tresses in the steamy spring. She closed her eyes, wishing she could have his hands on her forever. He took his time washing her hair and finger-combing thick bundle, and he piled the mass atop her head in a tight bun. Nadia smiled gratefully.

"After we get done with this class, I'd like to help you get Perry whatever publicity he needs."

"Now, I'm trying to play by your rules, but that sounds a lot like you're making longer term goals," he murmured. Nadia opened her mouth to protest, but was stopped in her tracks by the sound of gunfire.

~

Nadia pushed through the undergrowth with Lincoln following closely behind. She struggled into her clothes as she ran. He limped, wishing he could run, too. What had gone wrong in the handful of minutes he was with her at the hot springs? When they burst through the thicket at the edge of camp, he frantically surveyed the scene. Perry stood with his gun pointed at Rick's chest, a murderous glint in his eyes.

Nadia yelped and threw herself between them. Lincoln grabbed his wrist and wrestled the gun down. "Don't do this, buddy. This isn't the way," he pleaded.

Perry's blue eyes hardened as he stared at his nemesis. "I merely fired a warning shot. Showing Rick what happens to wolves when they come sniffing around our camp. I think he got the message."

"Loud and clear," Rick spat angrily. When he swiped his arm across his forehead, his hand shook, but he set his jaw. "You're making a big mistake. You lucked up on two prime students, but I happen to know your business has been in the red for a long time. I'm your best bet for giving Clyde MacAskill more than empty promises. Empty promises don't pay the bills."

"Sorry, but we don't live in the world of the hostile takeover," Perry murmured. "I listened to your proposal, and I turned it down. Now, I think I've been generous enough, even hearing you out. I suggest you get the hell out of my area before my generosity runs out."

Rick Feldman backed away. "Don't come crawling to me when the money runs out."

The three of them stared at the place where he had been standing as the bells echoed through the woods. Then, he was gone. Lincoln slowly exhaled and locked eyes with Nadia. They both looked at Perry. "What the hell happened?" Lincoln asked.

"He tried to strong arm me into going into business together."

"I gathered that much, but why did you try to shoot him?"

"I told you it was just a warning shot, and I pulled the gun because —I hate to admit it but—everything he said was right. I wanted to shut him up. Before this course, I hadn't had a class in months. It's the worst possible time for Clyde to be bedridden. Honestly, I don't know if he'll be well enough for another group to come through after you guys, and we're losing money like a leaky faucet." Perry sighed and ran a hand over his face.

"What can we do to help?" Lincoln asked.

Nadia's eyes it up. "I know! I have a team of people who handle my image. That's what you need, Perry! A PR team to rebrand you. And, with Lincoln's endorsement, you can target upmarket clients and increase the price of your courses."

"I do this to get away from words like 'rebranding' and 'upmarket'," Perry chuckled dryly. "I don't peddle pricy getaways to rich people looking for a unique travel experience. That's Rick's job. I started this business to teach everyday folks how to survive off the land."

"Perry, your business has to evolve in order to sustain itself," Lincoln replied quietly.

"There has to be a better, more authentic, way."

"There is," said Lincoln. "Why struggle to lure students month after month when you can reach an audience of millions on a weekly basis?" An idea began to take shape based on something Carmen had said on the phone back when he was lost in the woods. Nadia seemed to pick up on his line of thought.

"Oh, my gosh! You're brilliant!" she gasped.

Perry eyed them warily. "What are we talking about here?"

"I'm talking about your own television show," Lincoln replied. "Think of it. With the right team, the right pitch and my industry connections, we can make Survive Anything the number one show in America. You have the body, the look, the credentials!"

"Wait a minute, wait a minute. You can't be serious. Acting is your thing, not mine," Perry protested.

"And the wilderness is yours, but you brought us into your world and taught us how to make it. I'm not talking about acting. I'm talking reality. Reality TV."

"Give me your phone," Nadia commanded, moving with the momentum. She marched over to Perry's bags and dug out his cellphone. "I'm calling my assistant. She'll have everything arranged for us to meet with a branding specialist as soon as we make it back to civilization."

"I think I know who to tap for a production like this." Lincoln bubbled with excitement as Perry shook his head in disbelief. His stunned expression morphed to one of extreme happiness. It was like watching the sun come up. Nadia moved to the round lodge to chat with her assistant while Lincoln pondered how to convince Carmen to get her father onboard.

Perry sat down by the fire and said, "I can't believe you guys are doing this. Just know, if it doesn't work out, I really do appreciate the gesture."

"But, if it does work out, would you do it?" Nadia asked as she ended her call. Perry shrugged, committing to nothing.

"You have to, Perry. You've kind of grown on us," Lincoln joked.

Perry lifted his eyes to him. "That's what I'm worried about," he said.

That week, as Perry taught health and well-being, he tried not to think of Nadia and Lincoln's lofty plans for him. Their suggestion of a reality TV show came from a place of good intentions but impracticality. Even if they managed to find a network willing to give him a chance, Perry was not sure he wanted to dive into the world of rabid fans, paparazzi and constant scrutiny. He valued his privacy more than most.

He was right at home in the woods and, to that end, he pretended the conversation by the campfire had never happened. He handed out pocket-sized guidebooks about medicinal herbs and plants and told them to guard it with their lives. He showed them how to make teas, tinctures and salves for common ailments. There were lectures on how to set broken bones along with ones on how to handle stomach aches and joint pain.

Using sinew with needles fashioned from bone, he taught them how to do rudimentary stitches for bad cuts and gashes and how to apply natural antibiotic ointment like spruce sap to speed healing. He also taught them how to recognize a medical crisis that required immediate outside help.

Perry hammered home what he considered the most important survival skill which was attentiveness and that lesson was driven home later that week when Lincoln was bathing alone in the hot springs. He returned to camp in a rush, breathing heavily. "There was someone in the woods," he announced.

Perry was suddenly on high alert. "What did you see?"

"Some guy with a cellphone. I think he was taking pictures or videos of me."

"Didn't you hear the alarms?" Perry asked. Lincoln held up the length of cord Perry had strung with bells. The ringers were removed. "Damn it! This is getting out of hand. Let's check the perimeter and see how much of our system has been compromised."

"You are thinking that it was Rick?" Nadia rubbed her shoulders and looked around fearfully. Perry squared his jaw as he marched into the woods without answering her. He was certain it was Rick or someone from his crew. Someone who thought snagging nude photos of a celebrity was fair game.

Lincoln limped along with him. "Tabloids will spend thousands for an image like that. Hell, I've been ass out in a bunch of movies, but if they're watching me, it's only a matter of time before they realize Nadia is who they should really be watching."

"I know," Perry sighed as her eyes widened with concern. "But I'm not gonna let that happen. Stay here, Nadia. Let us see if anyone else is lurking in the woods."

"Thank you," she said.

Perry wanted to take the war to Rick Feldman. For his clients' sake, he had to keep his temper in check. But the incident was another reminder on the long list of reasons fifteen minutes of fame was not on his bucket list. He would find another way to save Survive Anything.

He and Lincoln loped off to check the rest of the perimeter bells. They discovered that a section of the line had been cut, offering a point of entry where a lurker could get by undetected. Perry stared at the breach. The land was public, so there was no legal way to go after Rick, or anyone else, for trespassing.

He knew the rival instructor was just trying to undermine him to make it seem as if he could not protect his students. Normally, for someone like Lincoln Easley, a breach of privacy would be a deal breaker, and Rick seemed to be banking on Lincoln trashing Perry's reputation. Luckily, Rick did not understand the nature of their relationship.

"While this is going on, I think we better stay close to camp. Nadia's gonna hate staying away from the hot springs, though," Lincoln said.

Perry chuckled. "Forget the hot springs. We've got a hot tub. We're finishing the course at the cabin instead of in the woods. Everything else I have to teach you guys can be done indoors."

"Are you serious?" Lincoln asked. Perry nodded. The actor balled his fists triumphantly and shook them at the sky. "Thank you, Rick Feldman!"

Laughing, they trekked back to camp and told Nadia their plans. Perry was not sure which of them looked more relieved. "But it's too late to move out tonight," said Perry. "We'll get everything ready to return to the cabin in the morning."

They gathered their belongings and packed extra food, and Perry suspended the backpack from a tree to keep wolves and bears away. By nightfall, they sat around the campfire, spirits buoyed by the turn of events.

"I can't wait to mail these letters off to Maria when we get there," Nadia said.

"You're looking forward to mail. I'm looking forward to a decent meal. I'm probably not gonna know what to do with myself when I taste salt again," Lincoln said.

Perry leaned back on his elbows and gazed up at the tree branches above. "I'll check on Clyde when we get back. He needs to know what Rick has been up to."

"Why is Rick so hell-bent on running your business into the ground?"

"It's a long story."

"The night is young," Lincoln said with a grin.

"We went to high school together, played football together. I was a natural, and he struggled. I excelled academically, and he struggled. I became a SEAL, but when I retired from the military, I was damn near broke, unemployed. I shunned family and friends who could have helped me get re-accustomed to civilian life."

"That had to be hell," said Lincoln.

"Rick had Empowered Survival, and he was doing well. So, Clyde convinced me to start Survive Anything to teach real bush-craft. Unfortunately, Rick took it as one more thing I was trying to do better than him."

Nadia rolled her eyes. "Boys will be boys."

"I never intended for the rivalry to affect the two of you," said Perry. "For that, I'm sorry. Rick will learn the hard way. I destroy anything that tries to come between me and the people I care about." He swept Nadia's hair back from her face, and her lips trembled as he softly kissed her. Dark eyes met blue ones, emotion glistening like stars and suns in their depths.

Nadia seemed to realize they were out in the open. She pulled back shyly. Perry bit his lip and nodded as she turned to Lincoln, clearing her throat. "So, how's that ankle feeling?" she asked, a little too brightly.

"I care about you, too," Lincoln said with a grin.

She heaved a shaky sigh and laughed. "Don't tell me this is the part where we talk feelings. Because I thought we established this is just something to do while we're out here. My dad would kill me if he found out."

"I'm rapidly developing a distaste for your dad," Lincoln said teasingly.

"Come on. Let's get to bed. It's late," Perry replied.

They retired to the round lodge, and Perry stood at the door, and stared into the woods for several minutes. When he was sure that no one lurked in the shadows, he secured the door and stretched out in the bough bed. Sleep was the furthest thing from Perry's mind.

CHAPTER 14

Nadia cupped Lincoln to her neck and Perry to her breast. As one man swept silky kisses into the valley of her cleavage, the other kissed her racing pulse. Her spine arched. Lincoln's questing hand snaked to the V between her legs, and he petted her warm, moist pussy. He slipped a finger inside, knowing she yearned to be filled with more. She was practically begging for it.

The trio had tried sleeping, but the need for release was too strong. Nadia wanted to drag out the blissful night and make it last forever. She wondered how to handle being double-teamed by two expert lovers. She damn sure had no complaints as pleasure spiraled higher and higher within her.

The wicked fulfillment intensified when Perry kissed his way over the hills of her breasts to her flat, quivering stomach. Meanwhile, Lincoln turned his attention to sipping the moans of excitement from her lips. She split her focus between the two of them.

Perry brushed the tip of his nose over her soft, curly pubic hairs, and Nadia nervously covered herself. But he stared at her with eyes that said she had nothing to hide. "Open for me," he coaxed. As he dropped butterfly kisses over her quivering inner thighs, her legs fell open. His fingertips skimmed her aching body with the barest caress.

His mouth parted the petals of her womanhood. She arched off the bough bed with a cry as he flicked his tongue first one way, then the other. Her mouth hung open in utter shock at the rapture. "Yes!" she whispered. Clutching the back of his head, she guided him to the pulsating nub of her clit where he swirled lazy circles with his tongue, taunting and teasing her. "Ooh, yes!" she gasped.

Perry dove his tongue into her fountain. He shamelessly fucked her with the velvety pink spear. Her pelvis rocked back and forth with the tilt of his head, and she felt her nectar gliding down her slit as her arousal skyrocketed. He nibbled and nipped at her clit, making her whine in ecstasy. Lincoln spread her labia to give him greater access, and Nadia bucked wildly against Perry's face.

"I want to make you mine," Lincoln whispered. He suckled her pert brown nipple, his mouth sending a wave of pleasure from her aching breasts to her core. Fine tremors wracked her body in response as his hot tongue fluttered from globe to globe. She could hardly stand it, especially in conjunction with what Perry was doing.

Nadia was an instrument that they both played skillfully, and all she could do was hum her delight. "What are you doing to me? Oh, God! Yes!" She thrashed her head as Perry finally relented.

"I have to be inside of you," he growled.

Perry dragged her into his lap, and she felt the bulge of his erection. They were, all three, naked. Sparks of awareness shot through her as he captured her mouth in a searing kiss. He shoved a hand between their bodies and guided his cock into her saturated womanhood. Nadia was familiar with his primal passion. His first powerful thrust jostled her in his arms, and she clung to his neck.

Lincoln kneeled behind her, masturbating against the crease of her ass. His feverish kisses spilled sighs of anticipation along her skin. "You feel so good," he hissed. She shivered at his grunt of ecstasy. They made no secret of how much she turned them on.

Perry grabbed her hips and anchored her to his pelvis, spearing into her quaking pussy, and her grip tightened reflexively. Erogenous zones she had never known flared to life with his every stroke. Nadia stammered his name in staccato moans as he pounded her apex and scraped against her clit. At the same time, Lincoln toyed with her asshole.

She started to climax, and she could not stop. She squeezed him with her knees, arms locked around his neck, as she latched on tighter and rocked on waves of exhilaration. A high-pitched, keening cry broke free of her throat. Perry tried to cover her mouth, but it barely muffled the sound. Her inner muscles rippled with spasms of pleasure, each one more intense than the last. She looked down, and her thighs were drenched from her gush of ecstasy.

Perry threw back his head and yanked out of her warm embrace before he exploded. "Mmph!" he sighed roughly. Within seconds, Lincoln took his place, pushing her forward and plunging into her wetness from behind. Nadia clutched Perry's shoulders. She stared into his awestruck eyes. He channeled a powerful desire to please her. His textured palm caressed her breasts in swift circles as she bounced in counter-thrust to Lincoln.

"How can I get enough of you?" he whispered. "How could anyone get enough of you?" He clasped her chin and kissed her with more tenderness than she had ever known. There was something in his touch that spoke even louder than his words.

She squeezed her eyes shut. *I'm not falling*, she warned herself. *I'm not! This is just sex.* But Lincoln gathered her in his arms and turned her onto her back. He stretched atop her nubile body, thrusting inside with a possessiveness she welcomed. In and out, he circled and swayed his hips, branding every part of her.

As he rose and fell between her legs, he sobbed her name like a prayer or an exultation. He masterfully took her back up the mountaintop, and she realized this was not their usual. He was making love to her. His lips never left her skin. He kissed and indulged her every fantasy as he tightened his buttocks, ramming deeper. It was a hard, penetrative confession that she could not ignore.

∾

Lincoln floated in the river of her orgasm. Her nectar covered his shaft in glistening wetness. Her explosive vocalizations thrilled every inch of him and made his erection harder. She wrapped her long, shapely legs around his waist and locked her heels behind his thighs. She clasped his taut ass cheeks to guide him. They ground together in slow, heated wonder.

Sweat beaded on his brow as he tried not to climax, but she felt like heaven in his arms. He loved her softness, her scent, her fire. He made eye contact with Perry, who seemed to be thinking the same thing: *There was no coming back from this.* Whatever happened when they left this forest, they were all irrevocably changed by the experience.

Her silky pussy enveloped him like a soft, moist cloud. As he pulled out, she dragged him in. He fought for control, but the power was in her hands. Her perky breasts skimmed his chest and made his heart race. "Nadia..." Lincoln pleaded. Her spine arched as her pelvis canted forward to take him even deeper. "Ooh! You're gonna make me give it all to you..."

"Not *all* of it," Perry chuckled seductively. He painted Lincoln's parted lips with the tip of his throbbing hard-on. A drizzle of pre-cum dripped from Lincoln's mouth before he swept his tongue out to catch it, and Perry leaned forward to kiss him and taste himself.

Suddenly, Nadia's slender fingers curled around his impressive cock. He flinched with need as she whispered, "You can both give it all to me." She tilted her head back and took him into her mouth. His beautiful shaft disappeared inch by inch past her rosy lips. The wickedly erotic tableau made Lincoln tremble and strain against her.

"Nadia! Hmm, Nadia!" Perry gasped. His heaving chest gleamed in the darkness. His muted growl stirred deeper arousal within Lincoln who groaned, staring at him plunge in and out of her mouth. Perry's glistening shaft was ridged and engorged, and he visibly throbbed. The muscular survivalist helplessly shoved his fingers through his hair as his pelvis jerked forward.

Nadia greedily hummed around his cock. She was glorious. Her pale skin glowed. Her hourglass figure was a masterpiece. Her cheeks hollowed, and she sucked Perry more aggressively. "Oh, God!" Lincoln moaned as he stared at her. The slick sound of her oral sex made him clasp her upper thighs and pound out his amazement. His jaw dropped at the mind-blowing pleasure. He rose on his knees to bring Perry's lips to his, and they kissed as Perry rode her face.

"*Fuck*," he huffed.

"Let me taste you. I need to taste you," Lincoln panted.

"How bad do you need it?" Perry ground out.

His blue eyes shot sparks as he asked the question. In response, Lincoln dove his tongue into his mouth again in a kiss that was hard and promising. Then, he dropped his head and took over for Nadia. She kissed his chin as if begging for another taste, while he wrapped his lips around Perry's shaft and let his tongue swirl over the head of his cock.

This is the definition of madness, Lincoln thought.

They were mad for each other. He could not slake his desire, no matter what they did. His pleasure plateaued, only to peak again seconds later, and he knew no one else could do this for him—not like Nadia and Perry, together. Lincoln was shocked to learn a polyamorous relationship could be everything he ever wanted and needed in the bedroom. But could the fire last beyond the forest?

Groaning, he peered up at Perry masturbating over him. The tension in the round lodge neared the breaking point, but Lincoln pushed boundaries. He wanted it to be the best release either of them had ever had.

He felt it in his bones. He heard it in Perry's breathless whispers of affirmation. It tightened in Nadia's pussy as she gripped him and rippled around his erection. *Come for me*, Lincoln mentally coaxed. Her musical whimpers increased in volume as she tumbled closer to the edge of oblivion. She writhed beneath him, rocking her pelvis to meet his thrusts, cooing his name like a siren.

"Lincoln! Yes!" she shouted.

Her release crashed over him. Lincoln rode her body harder as he groaned around Perry's member. Toying with her clit, he drew out the magnificent bliss, and her ejaculation rained around his cock and gushed down his thighs. Her reddened face was the picture of completion as her shoulders jerked uncontrollably.

Perry suddenly shoved him away. "I'm gonna come," he grunted. "I want to be inside you when I come!" He quickly moved behind Lincoln and thrust inside.

"Perry!" he gasped. White hot shock zinged through his system, and he let out a strangled moan. But, despite the stunning shift in momentum, the pounding in his loins was unstoppable. He hitched in a breath as Perry drilled him faster and harder in pursuit of the lightning. He felt Perry's spunk dribble out of his tight asshole and spill over his balls; yet, still he hammered. "Huhn! Ah, God!"

And the dam holding back Lincoln's climax released. He jerked out of Nadia's body at the last minute. His jizz sprayed from his dick in an explosive stream. The orgasm tore through his core with the power of a thousand stars igniting. A broken whimper escaped him as he collapsed on top of her with Perry planted deep within his body.

"Fuck, Lincoln! Oh, fuck," Perry sobbed.

Fingers twitching, Lincoln clutched the dry leaves of the bough bed and tried to stay conscious. "I can't walk away from this," he moaned. Tremors wracked his body as he continued erupting on Nadia's quivering stomach. She wrapped her arms around him. "I can't..." He shuddered. It was the most intense orgasm he had ever had.

Perry slowly fell away from him, and Lincoln tried to move. But his sated body rebelled. He fell asleep on Nadia's chest with Perry's arm draped over them both. Lincoln never wanted to leave.

"**W**ake up. We have a problem," Perry muttered. He patted Lincoln on the shoulder and rested on his haunches until the actor and Nadia opened their eyes. Perry hiked a thumb in the direction of the lodge door. "Someone took our things in the night."

"What?" Lincoln blinked groggily.

Moments later, Perry led them to the tree where they had suspended their belongings. The cord was cut. He gestured at broken underbrush. "Two or three men. I'm guessing from Rick Feldman's camp."

Nadia threw her hands up in disbelief. "We can't let them get away with this."

"Our food, water, weapons, first aid gear and my cellphone were in the pack," Perry sighed. "But we can't afford to go after Rick. We're stuck out here with no communication and none of the tools we need to get by. We need to get back to the cabin as soon as possible. It's too dangerous out here without gear."

"Wait a minute." Nadia slipped into the round lodge and swept aside her bedding. She found the notebook with her letters and Lincoln's sketchbook and brought them out with a sigh of relief. "Thank goodness, they didn't take this. My notebook can't get into the wrong hands."

"Please tell me there's nothing incriminating in your letters," Lincoln pleaded.

She protectively clutched her notebook to her chest.

"That's unimportant right now. Got your knives?" Perry asked as he turned away from putting out the fire. Lincoln touched his waist-band, and Nadia whipped hers from the top of her boot. "Alright, we don't have time to waste. Let's get going."

They were stranded in the woods with nothing but the clothes on their backs and their hunting knives. Perry gazed up at the sky through the trees and noted the pallid sky touched by the first rays of dawn. If they made good timing, they would arrive at the cabin around midday, and Perry could figure out what to do about Rick.

He understood exactly what his rival was doing, but this time things had gone way too far.

Lincoln was hampered by his injured ankle and Perry was forced to call breaks every hour. He was grateful the descent was easier than the climb and at least the weather was on their side, a breezy late autumn day with only a hint of winter chill.

Nadia gasped and pointed excitedly. "Look at that!"

"Beautiful," Lincoln whistled. "Check out that waterfall."

"It's actually a cascade," said Perry. "Let's take another break and grab a drink while we're here. We don't have much further to go." While they stopped for water, Perry studied Lincoln's face, noting the tense straightness of his lips and pain clouding his emerald eyes. "How are you holding up?"

"I'm managing." Lincoln smiled.

Perry knelt before him and checked the splint he had rewrapped at camp. The swelling was down, but the joint was warm and inflamed. "When we get to the cabin, I'll take care of you," he promised. He clasped his forearm and dragged him to his feet.

"I like the sound of that," Lincoln said. "Remind me to show Rick my appreciation for trying to make our lives miserable. He only succeeded in bringing us closer together."

"Oh, make no mistake. I have something for Rick, and it isn't 'appreciation,'" Perry chuckled.

It was just after noon when he spotted the cabin rooftop through the trees. The sight of it seemed to galvanize all three of them. Taking stumbling steps down the hillside, they sped along to the familiar front door. Perry unlocked it and led them into the quiet, cozy house.

"Make yourselves at home!"

"Hey, where do you keep the *non-foraged* food?" Nadia raced straight to the kitchen and returned with a box of crackers and cheese, a bottle of soda water. Perry smiled at her exuberance as she threw herself in an armchair and took the first bite with a dreamy sigh. "So good," she crooned.

"Pass it along," said Lincoln, settling on the living room couch. She made him a cheese and crackers sandwich and sauntered over to him. She straddled his lap seductively and placed the food to his lips. Lincoln grinned and kissed her fingertips, after he ate the bite.

"I'll start up the hot tub for you guys," Perry said as he stepped through a sliding patio door to tinker with the machine. He wanted to make them comfortable. More than that, he wanted to keep them preoccupied while he did what he had to do. Rick Feldman would regret the day he ever stepped foot in Perry's camp.

CHAPTER 15

An hour later, Nadia luxuriated in the bubbling hot tub. She had eaten and taken a shower, something she had not realized how much she missed until the steamy water hit her skin. She had dropped her letters for Maria in the mailbox just as the mail truck stopped by. She had called her assistant to make sure the meeting was still on between her team and Perry Evans, and she had left a message for her father to let him know she was safely back at the cabin.

She nuzzled Lincoln's neck and snuggled closer as the water floated them to arousal. He was freshly shaved, and smelled like soap. His wavy hair was clean and silky, it glistened in the sunlight. She sighed with contentment. The only thing missing was Perry; he was somewhere inside the house.

When they locked eyes, Nadia shivered at the obvious affection she saw in Lincoln's gaze. "Cold?" he asked, pulling her closer.

"No, just thinking. I can't stand the thought of us saying goodbye at the end of the week. But, my father…"

"Forget what your father wants. What do you want?"

Smiling with regret, she let her hand trail over his muscular chest, down to his smooth, hard erection. "We both know you can't always get what you want," she whispered. He eased her astride his cock, pushing inside of her with a soft exhale.

"That doesn't stop us from craving. What do you want, Nadia Marson?"

His lips coasted over her mouth. She hitched in a breath at the tantalizing coils of pleasure tightening as he began moving with unhurried thrusts. He glided in and out of her satiny pussy, and he stroked a fire to life. She wrapped her arms around his neck and bracketed him between her legs.

She chose to ignore the question. Tried to ignore his questing eyes. But she could not ignore his undemanding kisses. She let the water rock her in his arms and bring her against his sexy hard body. His manhood plumbed her depths. His lips coasted over her mouth again, and she hitched in a breath as a hint of vulnerability flitted across his face.

"Say it," he said quietly.

"You know what I want."

She gripped him tighter. He buried his fingers in the hair at the base of her skull, and his burning mouth skimmed over the pale mounds of her breasts. "I want to hear it," he whispered.

Melting in ecstasy, Nadia let her head loll back. What would happen if she caved in? She could tell him she wanted him. She wanted Perry. They had no chance, but she wanted them. In fact, she was falling in love with them, but she could not say that.

"I want this," she whimpered.

"Then, we do whatever it takes," he said. "I don't want to lose you. How do either of you expect me to give this up?"

Her body molded to his, and everything he said made sense. But she knew it was the foolish kind of sense that was only reasonable in the heat of the moment. With a growl of rapture, he clasped her hips and drove her up and down on the long, hard spear of his cock. As the sex intensified, the water splashed over the edge of the tub.

They writhed together, locked in bliss, but she struggled to understand what he was trying to say. So, he did not want to 'give this up.' In the woods, he had said he cared about them. Perry had said it, too.

Neither of them had mentioned the L-word. *Love.* She had too much at stake to risk it all for a good time. *But, damn, isn't it good,* she thought.

Suddenly, Nadia's insides quaked in release. "Lincoln! Yes!" she cried out. Lincoln remained buried to the hilt, and the intensity her climax took him over the edge. He went stiff, shuddered. She felt his orgasm blossom in her garden.

"Oh, my God!" he gasped. "Nadia!"

He buried his face in the crook of her neck and squeezed her close as he poured out everything he had to give. She went limp in his arms, sated. Even as they recovered, she did not want to move. She rested her head on his shoulder and listened to him breathe, felt his heart beating against her chest. Her throat burned with unshed tears.

"You have a career to get back to in LA, and Perry needs to get Survive Anything on track. You know my situation. With everything at stake, why would we fight to keep this going?" she whispered.

Lincoln leaned back and looked her in the face. "Because we're in love with each other, Nadia."

Nadia studied him closely to see if he was just saying what she wanted to hear, but he looked serious. The house phone rang before she could ask further questions. "Perry will get it," she murmured. It was a bad time for interruptions. No one moved inside the house, however. Nadia half-rose and peered through the patio door.

"Is he in there?" Lincoln asked as the phone rang again.

"I'll go check." She got out of the hot tub and grabbed a fluffy towel from a hook on the cabin wall. She slipped inside where the heater and fireplace warmed the room to a comfortable temperature. Perry was nowhere in sight. She absently picked up the phone, taking one last look around. "Hello?"

"Nadia?"

"Dad! Hey, I called you an hour or two ago. We made it back to the cabin. We came in early."

"Yes, I got your message," said Wilson Marson. "In fact, I was pleased to hear you came in early. I took the liberty of arranging a car service to pick you up. You'll be at the airport by later this evening and home before morning."

"No, I think you misunderstood me, Dad. I have another week left before the training course is over. We agreed I can stay here until it's done."

"Nadia, what's one week going to change? I need you at the lab. I've already made arrangements. You're coming home."

Nadia stood her ground, thinking of Lincoln's confession in the hot tub. "*No*, I'm not. I can't. I'm thinking about investing in a business venture with my instructor."

"Excuse me? You've been out there two weeks with him, and you're ready to throw money at him?" Wilson said in disbelief.

Nadia explained, "Perry's survival training course doesn't have the reach it could have if he packaged it in television format. The other student, Lincoln Easley, happens to know a thing or two about how the entertainment industry works. I want to help. I know I can do this. You just have to...trust me."

"You will not have my backing on this. I raised you better than this. I raised you to be *smarter* than this."

She swallowed the lump in her throat and fought tears. "Cancel the car service. I'll—I can make my own way home when I'm good and ready." She dropped the phone into the cradle with a dejected sigh. She had stood up to her father, and it felt exactly like she thought it would. Like defeat.

Lincoln tucked a towel around his hips and limped into the house. The therapeutic effect of the hot tub had taken away some of the pain in his ankle, but he was grateful for a soft couch and a warm fire. He slumped on the sofa and turned on the television.

The news channel filled the room with the cautious voice of a meteorologist. He raised a brow and increased the volume. "...Everyone in our viewing area to take this weather event seriously.

We'll see extremely heavy snow and damaging winds beginning tomorrow."

"Nadia," Lincoln called out. "Is he in here?"

She appeared at the living room door, eyes sad and weary. "No, I don't think so. He must've gone somewhere while we were in the hot tub, probably to town to pick up some supplies."

"Watch this," Lincoln gestured at the forecast.

The meteorologist stood before a map covered in blue and purple. A split-screen showed a city blanketed by a few feet of snow, and the image transitioned to cars slowly crawling along an icy highway past a bad pile-up. Nadia crossed her arms and moved closer with a frown.

Lincoln shook his head in dismay as the meteorologist continued, "A wintry mix of rain and snow has already developed to the west, but we're seeing a low-pressure system rapidly intensifying to our south, meaning this weather will stall right over much of our viewing area. Authorities are telling residents to stay inside."

Nadia gestured at the television. "What's that mean for us?"

"I don't know, but I hope we have enough food and firewood. We're gonna be stuck in here for a while. Maybe Perry saw it coming and got out to restock." Lincoln made his way to the guestroom to get dressed. She followed him, sitting at the foot of his bed, watching with curious brown eyes.

"I'm glad I just turned down a flight home from my dad."

"What about the job offer?"

She rubbed her temple and looked away with a tired sigh. "You said yourself that we have to do whatever it takes. I told him about the television idea for Perry, and he immediately assumed I was blowing my money on a shitty investment."

Lincoln hummed sympathetically as he settled beside her. "Reminds me of how my parents reacted when I told them I wanted to go to Hollywood."

"I'm scared," Nadia admitted. "Without my dad's support, I'll go broke before I can do anything substantial to help Perry. I was honestly counting on him to lend his support."

"He'll come around," said Lincoln. "And, if he doesn't, don't worry about it. We have a plan. We know this isn't a bad investment. Prove it to your father and remember, you're not alone in this."

"Thanks for the reminder. I needed it." She wrapped her arms around him in a tight hug and inhaled the scent of his cologne, comforted by his words. "Now, come on. We have to prepare for this bad weather. The last time I ignored a storm warning, I ended up stranded in a category three hurricane."

"I wonder when Perry will make it back," Lincoln mused aloud.

While they waited for him, they took stock of what was in the kitchen pantry. There was a modest supply of nonperishables, but not enough to last more than a few days. It made Lincoln nervous, but he tried to hide the fact.

"Well, there's a gas range, at least...in case the power goes out," Nadia noted.

"You want to look around and see if you can find oil lamps or candles? We don't want to be stuck in the cold and dark when the lights go out."

"God, I hope it doesn't get that bad," Nadia murmured.

"I'll go make sure there's enough firewood," he called out.

The temperature had already begun dropping and the wind was picking up. The sky was a shade of mottled grey that promised heavy snow. Lincoln noticed a neat stack of logs against the side of the cabin and another pile that needed splitting. He grabbed the ax and got to work, but his mind was on Perry's whereabouts.

The Jeep was still in the garage, he noticed. Perry could not have gone to town. Lincoln glanced at the kitchen window where he saw Nadia refilling a rustic old lamp from a bottle of lamp oil. He decided not to tell her about his growing concerns regarding their instructor.

Lincoln shaded his eyes and gazed up the mountainside. *Don't tell me he went back up to pick a fight with Rick.* He swung the ax again. The sharp blade connected with a *thwack,* and two roughly equal halves of wood tumbled to the cold, hard ground. He pushed himself to work faster.

About an hour later, a light drizzle started up, and Lincoln's uneasiness skyrocketed. Perry still was not back. Nadia was in the cabin with limited food and resources, and he had a sprained ankle. The situation was getting serious fast.

~

Perry entered the cabin followed by a blustery gust of snow. The blazing fire sputtered in the fireplace as icy wind ripped through the room. Perry slammed the door behind him.

"Fuck!" he swore, shivering. When he turned around, Lincoln hugged him like he had been gone a thousand years. Perry's eyes widened in surprised pleasure, and he slowly wrapped his arms around him. "Nice to see you, too."

"Where the hell have you been?" Lincoln countered, pushing away. "We were worried sick! I thought you were stuck in the goddamned blizzard. I even called nine-one-one, but they told me first responders were only coming out for emergencies."

"I was, uh..." Perry shrugged out of his coat and eased the gloves from his fingers, face burning from the cold. "I was with the park rangers." He ambled to the fireplace to work the chill out of his bones. Nadia trailed him, clasping his hands in hers.

"You're damn near frozen," she whispered. Her warm touch delivered comfort as she traced his cold palms. she ushered him to the loveseat. Lincoln settled beside him, while she took the armrest.

Perry studied them, realizing they both looked like the strain of trying to figure out where he had gone had taken a toll on them. He regretted leaving without telling them. He simply had not expected things to go the way they had gone.

"We were worried you went after Rick," Lincoln said.

"I was halfway there," Perry admitted. "Then, one of the park rangers spotted me and told me about the snow storm. Rick had broken camp already. We had no way to hear about the changing conditions since he stole our gear, but he knew the weather was about to take a turn for the worse.

"We're talking a storm of the century. Last time we got weather like this, the power went out region-wide, roads were closed for days, and people died. Apparently, deputies are going door-to-door, telling people in isolated pockets like this one to evacuate."

"It sounds like you're saying that heartless bastard Rick Feldman tried to get us killed," Lincoln said.

Perry furrowed his brow, having considered the same thought. "I say we refrain from speculating about Rick's motives. The bottom line is, I called the sheriff and told him what Rick did to us. We'll let the authorities deal with that problem. Now, we have a new problem. It's too late for the three of us to leave here by Jeep. The snow is coming, and it's dark. We have to ride out the storm."

"We checked the pantry. I don't think we have enough food for a long stay," Lincoln murmured.

"We have at least enough for a week," Perry pointed out.

Nadia waved her hands and marched over to the house phone. "I can have a helicopter get us out of here."

"No one will fly in this weather." The phone fell into the cradle with an ominous click, and Nadia crossed her arms and gnawed on her plush bottom lip fearfully. Perry was unnerved, too, but they could handle this.

He gravitated to the patio door and peered out, noting that someone had transferred the firewood from outdoors to indoors. Perry was grateful one of them had taken the initiative. Nadia's mouth straightened in a firm, resolute line as she stepped up beside him.

"Tell me one thing, and be straight with me," she said. "How worried should we be?"

"If it was up to me, I'd get you two out of here fast as lightning, but it's not up to me. We're in it for the long haul. So, we'll run the heater while we have power and conserve the firewood as much as possible. We'll go easy on our food and water." Perry managed a rueful half-smile. "But we'll be fine. I promised I'd teach you how to survive anything. We can survive this."

"Then, what's the game plan?" she asked.

Perry turned away from the storm raging beyond the frosted glass and led his charges to the kitchen. "We continue with business as usual," he said. "Our last week of coursework centers on self-defense training. We'll start that tomorrow. Tonight, we take a break. I think we could all use some down time. Who's up for a dinner of something other than coon, rabbit or squirrel?"

Some of Nadia's fearfulness faded away as he took charge of the situation. The art of distraction was working. Perry helped Lincoln get dinner started while Nadia searched the pantry for hot cocoa. When she was out of earshot, Lincoln leaned close and whispered, "How long do you think we'll be stuck here?"

"Once the snow stops, I have a snowmobile in the barn to take you guys back to town. I say we enjoy this little time to ourselves." They locked eyes, and Perry saw the spark ignite. Lincoln knew exactly what he was talking about. Hot chocolate and even hotter nights in a cabin in the snow-blanketed woods. It sounded like bliss.

CHAPTER 16

The wind howled and shrieked, and the sky was lost in a grey-white haze, but the heater blew full-blast. A small fire burned in the fireplace. Inside the cozy cabin, Perry used the enforced confinement to take Nadia and Lincoln through some jujitsu moves.

"Again," he said. Nadia stepped out and brought her arms over her head. Perry tapped her stomach to encourage her to tighten her core. He moved to Lincoln and ran a hand down his thigh, bending his knees some. "Very good."

They practiced take-downs for another few hours. As a cool draft swept along the floor, Perry reveled in the feel of his lovers' bodies against his. What should have been exclusively self-defense training also turned into intimate caress-and-fondling training.

It was late noon when they stopped, but the raging storm made it seem closer to midnight. Perry finally collapsed beneath Lincoln's lithe frame and chuckled softly as his lover stole a kiss. Giggling, Nadia dropped on Lincoln's back, and both men groaned as if her slight weight was unbearable.

"When do you think the snow will stop?" she asked, rolling away.

Perry rested his face on the palm of his hand. "I have no idea. Want some lunch?"

"I have a taste for something," Lincoln murmured, "but it's not food."

"Get your mind out of the gutter. We need to eat. Can you toss another log on the fire?" Perry tapped his chest and rose to his feet.

Another log clunked into the fireplace, sending up sparks. Lincoln dusted his hands and followed Perry to the kitchen while Nadia stayed in the living room. "We're gonna run out of firewood," Lincoln observed.

"We'll make a move when the snow lets up. I'll be glad when I can get you two safely out of here."

Lincoln wrapped his arms around him from behind. "And after that?" he asked.

"What do you mean?" Perry opened a can of tomato soup and upended it over a pot as Lincoln massaged his shoulders.

"After we leave. Will you let Nadia and I make you a celebrity?"

Perry shrugged away from him and grabbed a loaf of bread, cracked the fridge a fraction and retrieved the cheese. "You two have to give up this notion of saving me. If my business tanks, I'll find something to do. Maybe go work at, say the supermarket or the post office. This little town has things to do."

Lincoln tucked a finger under his chin and forced him to meet his gaze. "Nadia stood up to her dad for you." There was silence as they both absorbed what that meant, but Perry shook his head and went back to fixing lunch.

"It doesn't matter because her father will never support her doing anything other than what he tells her to do."

Nadia stepped into the kitchen. "Luckily, I learned I don't need my father's permission to go after what I want. What about you? What's holding you back?"

Perry smiled wryly as he buttered the skillet and dropped slices of bread into the fragrant oil to make grilled cheese sandwiches. "The operative word in your statement is 'want.' I don't *want* to be famous. I can't fathom what it must be like to be the two of you—your lives are not your own." He blew out a breath.

When he turned around, two sets of eyes filled with disappointment stared at him. Nadia crossed her arms and was the first to look away. "Perry, this reality show will give us an excuse to be together a while longer to see if this works." She turned back to face him, her eyes full of challenge. "Or, maybe that's what you don't want?"

The knife he was holding clattered to the countertop as he turned back to the kitchen peninsula and dropped his head. "I know you're both all wrong for me," he said, almost to himself. "You're too cultured and coddled. If you had asked me two weeks ago if I wanted to be with someone like the two of you, the answer would have been no.

"But you've made me stare down wolves," he continued with quiet intensity. "I've chased you through the woods, and I've never chased a soul in my life. You make me wonder how the hell I can survive anything without you. So, don't pretend you don't know. I want to be with you."

"Then, get out of your comfort zone." Lincoln slipped between him and the kitchen countertop. "Do it for us. We'll help you make the transition. Besides, you won't get famous overnight," he chuckled. "You'll have plenty of time to adapt."

"I talked to my assistant," said Nadia. "Everything is all lined up. Next week, weather permitting, I can fly you out to Houston to meet a brand specialist. I'd love for you to meet my best friend Maria, as well. Both of you. She's read quite a bit about you."

"I knew you were writing about us," Lincoln stated.

Perry laughed and ran a hand over his face. "Alright, fine. I'll fly out to see you. I'll meet with your PR team and your best friend, and we'll pretend television producers are lining up around the corner to make another survivor show, which they aren't," he pointed out.

"They may not be, but I have a secret weapon," Lincoln confided. He threw an arm around each of them and pulled them closer. "I happen to know the daughter of one of reality TV's most powerful super-producers."

Nadia smiled conspiratorially. "This could work, guys. I can feel it. Who is she?"

"I met her on the set of *Vengeance with a Vengeance*, although she got her start in reality TV, too. Now she works for my agent, so I have a direct line to her. It's Carmen Wilde, the daughter of Herschel Wilde."

Nadia's face dropped. "I am *not* working with her!" She marched, fuming, to her bedroom.

~

The icy anger running through her veins rivaled the cold outside, and Nadia climbed into bed and drew the covers over her face. In her mind's eye, she saw Carmen—the smiling starlet on Jason Stratham's arm. She saw the tabloid headlines, the cameras and mics in her face.

She heard the snide questions she could not answer. *Did she know he was cheating? How did it feel being replaced by a reality TV star? What did her father think about her Wall Street fiancé leaving her for another woman?* The hurt and shame descended like an anvil, again.

Nadia had dated Jason for two years before discovering his final treachery. An entire two years of suspecting he was a cheater, but sticking around anyway. What hurt most after the breakup was the fact he was exactly the kind of man her father wanted her to marry—all front, business acumen, and conservative values.

His affair made Nadia feel like she had somehow failed at a game she never even wanted to play, let alone win.

She shook her head at the memories. She wanted to invest in Perry's future in television, but she wished she had known Lincoln's insider was the same woman who had landed her in the tabloids six months ago. *And what would you have done if you'd known? Would that have stopped you from trying to help Perry?* Nadia sighed.

The door to her bedroom opened quietly. She kept the covers over her face, but she felt the mattress depress. "You want to talk about it?"

Perry asked quietly. She shook her head, sniffed. "Same girl, huh?" She nodded. He gently tugged down the blanket.

"I'm sorry I overreacted. It just caught me off guard," she replied. He swept a tear from her cheek, and she cupped a hand over his. Lincoln stepped into view.

"It's my fault," he said. "If I had only known."

"Enough about the show," said Perry, softly and tenderly. "Making sure Nadia is okay is more important to me."

"I'm fine." Nadia sat up. "Honestly, I am. I feel nothing for Jason, and if I let my anger toward Carmen get in the way of us getting you a show, that means I'm letting what he did to me control me. I'm done letting anything or anyone control how I live my life."

Perry smiled. "Atta girl."

"Just make sure I never have to see her or talk to her."

Lincoln nodded, serious and earnest. "I'll do my best, promise."

"I'm kidding!" Nadia rolled her eyes at him. "But, seriously, I'm wondering if you guys really want to date a damaged billionaire," she quipped.

Lincoln laughed out loud, and Perry replied, "You're not damaged, honey. Someone broke your heart, and you built a wall, thinking that could stop you from getting hurt again. I did the same thing, and look where that got us."

"In a position," said Lincoln, "to learn it takes someone having your back when the pressure's on."

"What do you mean, Lincoln?" Nadia asked.

"I think he's trying to tell you we're not Jason," Perry stated. "You can trust us. Now, let's go grab a bite to eat while the food is still warm. No telling how long the electric will stay on, so don't count on the microwave. Come on."

Perry led them back into the main room of the house, and Nadia slowly walked over to the patio door. She pulled back the heavy drapes and she scrubbed away at the frost on the glass.

"Guys, the snow is halfway up the side of the cabin. How many feet is that? About three or four?"

"Mm-hmm. Do you like chives in your tomato soup?" Perry called out. It was then that the lights flickered several times before finally dying.

∾

The trio made a fort near the fire in the living room as it was the only source of heat. Perry and Lincoln chatted quietly on a pallet of blankets and quilts. Nadia curled on the sofa with her notebook on her knees. Lincoln ambled over to her and clutched her knees, peeling her legs apart. She fell back to the throw pillows invitingly.

"Writing more juicy stories about us?" he asked playfully. He kissed his way up her inner thighs to the happy place between her legs while she squirmed in pleasure.

"I'm not. I was simply writing to let Maria know how much she means to me."

He pulled a face.

"In case we don't make it out of this," she said soberly.

Perry and Lincoln shared a look, and Perry moved to the sofa to sit beside her. "Hey, what happened to believing we can survive anything?"

"I still believe that," she whispered.

Her voice held a tremor, despite her smile. They were all wearing their brave faces. Snow days were usually for vegging out with junk food while binge-watching TV, but supplies were too low for gratuitous eating and there was no TV. The snow was still falling, the power was out, and the firewood Lincoln and Perry had brought into the house would only last a few more days.

"I think it's time we tuck this princess in bed so she can stop worrying." Lincoln tugged her nightshirt over her head and removed it. She half-turned toward him, pale, satiny skin exposed.

Perry laced his fingers through her hair and gently drew her head back. His fiery lips blazed over Nadia's mouth, over her chin, down the side of her neck. "You don't have to be afraid, darling. We've got you," he murmured. His mouth covered hers, swallowing her soft whimper.

Lincoln sank to the floor and eased her panties aside. He tongue-kissed her snatch, letting the tip of his tongue sweep over her delicate anatomy. He buried his face between her legs. Her scent clouded his senses as he drowned in the smell of jasmine and roses and closed his mouth over her engorged clit, greedily sucking.

All the while, Perry guided his head up and down to satisfy her. Nadia's plaintive whimpers became breathless sobs for more. Her pelvis rocked ever faster against Lincoln's face, and she clutched Perry to her breasts.

Lincoln ran a hand over Perry's cock, and he jerked reflexively. Sliding a finger into Nadia's hot, tight snatch, Lincoln turned his attention to his other lover. He brought Perry's erection free and hummed with anticipation as he stared at the throbbing cock bouncing near his face.

Perry emitted a rough groan as Lincoln teasingly sucked the head of his erection. He wove his head back and forth, taking more and more of him with each approach. Finally, he let Perry slam to the back of his throat. Perry cried out and hugged him to his pelvis. He held still, afraid to move, afraid he would come.

Nadia slipped from the sofa. "Yes, bedtime sounds like a good idea," she whispered. She fluttered kisses over Lincoln's back as she drew him to the makeshift bed on the floor.

The pile of pillows cushioned them, and warm blankets kept away the chill. She parted her legs, and Lincoln stroked her deep and long with his two middle fingers as Perry rested on his knees next to them. She tightened around Lincoln's digits. He felt the minute tremors that signaled she was a ticking time bomb.

"Didn't he tell you, you're in good hands?" he asked seductively. Nadia moaned and canted her pelvis higher.

As she rode Lincoln's hand, Perry thrust into his mouth. Lincoln squeezed his eyes closed and groaned with anticipation. His dick hardened and lengthened in the loose lounge pants he had worn to bed. He took them off and let his beautiful member swing.

Lincoln touched himself. At the same time, he smoothly bobbed back and forth at Perry's cock with expert finesse. Perry's rod re-emerged glistening wet from his mouth, and the survival instructor brought him up and guided him to Nadia's body.

She eagerly wrapped around Lincoln like a vine. Her pelvis ground against his in search of completion, and her excitement took him to his back. Lincoln clutched her hips and let her ride him hard and fast. "Mmph! Nadia," he sputtered. His brow furrowed in ecstasy.

She writhed above him, while Perry positioned himself between the other man's legs. Lincoln moaned hoarsely as he eased inside. He gathered Nadia closer, giving Perry room to make love to him. It was mind-blowing to have her silky pussy caressing his rock-hard cock as Perry drilled him with slow, passionate mastery.

Perry touched something within him that made him want to let go. Every thrust pushed him closer to the edge, making him jerk and quiver in Nadia's pussy. Pre-cum mixed and mingled with her nectar between their legs, soaking them with lust.

Lincoln closed his eyes and his exhilaration climbed. Nadia whipped her hair over her shoulder and braced a hand against his muscular chest. Her heart-shaped ass slammed against Perry's stomach, and she looked back at him with unconcealed lust.

Growling, Perry leaned forward and kissed her hungrily as the three of them plowed together. She squeezed Lincoln with inner muscles that rippled around him from tip to base, milking him with slow precision. When one spasm ended, another began.

"Ooh, shit! Yes!" Lincoln gasped.

Perry's fingers dug into his thighs. Quaking tremors wracked him as the pleasure made his toes go numb from clenching them so tightly. He bucked against Nadia, against Perry. She stroked and he pounded, and Lincoln lay back and took it, lightheaded from the blood-rush to his dick.

"He's ready, baby," Perry grunted.

Lincoln hissed his name through clenched teeth and clutched the bedcovers as his lower body rose. Higher and higher, he hovered. He could not breathe for a few seconds. Spots swam before his eyes. Perry sent him higher, and Nadia brought the explosion.

"Hah!" Lincoln cried out.

He erupted inside of her, triggering her climax. He felt the blast strike the apex of her pussy and melt down around his pounding cock. Perry hugged his leg, kissing his inner knee and rocking harder and faster, and Lincoln felt him let go. They forgot about the storm. They climbed above the weather. Perry's chest heaved as he fell to the pile of blankets, and Nadia slumped in Lincoln's arms. The darkness closed peacefully around them, and they fell asleep.

CHAPTER 17

Nadia pressed her forehead to the door, trying to stay silent as she eavesdropped. Perry spoke quietly into the cellphone. "...Food for three more days, wood for two more... Trying to keep the students busy to keep their minds off the situation. Oh, and the power's out by the way."

Nadia squeezed her eyes shut as her heart sank. Suddenly, she was back at the resort with the hurricane screaming around her. Her temples pounded with the beginnings of a headache, and tension coiled in her neck and shoulders.

"Yeah, one injured," Perry said. "Makes it more difficult. Plus, I didn't think to require snow gear. This storm is way earlier in the season than usual. Sure, we can find something around here, but..."

She bit her bottom lip and tried to ignore her heart which was pounding with anxiety. Just the thought of trying to walk back to town made her want to curl up in a ball and hide. She remembered the short trek through the icy rain and shivered. Perry had to have a better plan than that. She strained to hear more of the conversation, but a sound behind her made her whip around.

"Everything okay?" Lincoln asked quietly.

"Perry isn't telling us everything."

"Don't give yourself a reason to worry, love."

Her eyes widened as Lincoln grabbed her wrist and ushered her away from Perry's door just as the survival instructor peered out. Nadia felt his blue eyes boring into their retreating backs. "You guys need something?" he asked.

"Nope, nothing at all," Lincoln called over his shoulder.

"Actually..." Nadia interjected. But Lincoln wrapped an arm around her to keep her from turning back. When they made it to the living room, he pressed her to the sofa.

"We should talk," he said.

"I don't want to talk! I want to *do* something. It's been two days since the storm started, and so much snow was dumped that the roads can't possibly be open. What are we going to do?"

"Perry has a snowmobile. He and I talked about it, but I didn't want to tell you, in case things went better than expected. He can take us to town one at a time. You can go first. I'll wait here."

"I'm scared," she said bleakly.

"I know," he whispered, sitting beside her and clasping her hands. "I'm scared, too. However, I trust Perry. He won't let us down. He'll get us out of this."

As Lincoln placated her, Perry quietly entered the room and grabbed his coat. "Where are you going?" Nadia pushed past Lincoln and confronted him at the door. She suppressed a scream of frustration when she caught the wary look that passed between the two men. They were trying to keep her from being anxious, but holding back information was not the way to do it.

"I'll be right back. I'm just stepping outside to the barn. Lincoln, why don't you see if there's anything to snack on in the pantry."

"There's not!" Nadia snapped. "And I'm not hungry. The oatmeal we ate for breakfast will tide me over. Besides, we don't have enough food to 'snack on' anything. Now, what's up?" No one said anything. Nadia put her hands on her hips and stared Perry down. "I heard you on the phone. I think we deserve to know how bad the situation has gotten."

Lincoln murmured, "She can handle it, Perry."

"Alright," Perry sighed. "The park offices were closed for the storm; so, we're on our own. I'm going to the barn to gas up the snow-mobile and get ready to transport you two to civilization."

She breathed a sigh of relief as she realized they would soon leave the mountain. "How long will it take us to get back to town via snow-mobile?" she asked.

Perry's face tightened. "It's a thirty-minute drive by car."

"Meaning, it'll take much longer by snowmobile," she surmised. "And it'll be much more dangerous since you can't see the roads. We might think it's solid ground beneath us and be coasting on nothing but powder."

Perry nodded. She hugged herself and turned away. Lincoln moved up behind her and squeezed her shoulders. "It's a risk we have to take. We can't stay here. It's already significantly colder in the house without the heater going, and the stove is fueled by a propane tank. Our fuel sources won't last much longer," he said.

"Since it's stopped snowing, can't I call for a helicopter?" she asked.

"Too dangerous," Perry replied. "With snow this fresh, the vibra-tion of the blades could easily set off an avalanche. Taking the snow-mobile is the safest option, even if it means a long ride in the cold. I know this area like the back of my hand. We'll be fine."

Perry wrapped his scarf around his face and moved to leave, but she stopped him with a hand to the arm. Nadia forced a smile. "Then, I'm coming with you to check on the snowmobile. I've been stuck in this cabin for days. Give me a second to suit up."

"You'll have more than a second," Lincoln replied as he slowly opened the front door. The three of them gaped at the wall of snow.

"I'll find the snow shoes," Perry mumbled.

∾

It took twenty minutes to dig a passage to the surface. Nadia rubbed her forearms. Perry knew her muscles burned from hauling snow to the bathtub and kitchen sink, since he suggested saving it in case they ran out of fresh water. When they emerged from the cabin into the whited-out world, she was awestruck by the surrounding scene. The sun reflected off the snow's surface with blinding brightness. Nadia shaded her eyes and looked around.

The air was dry and cold and smelled as clean and crisp as any she had ever breathed. Like the storm had washed the world.

"It's like we're the only people left," she murmured.

"Isolated as all hell." Perry eyed the beautiful, treacherous landscape with furrowed brow. "Hand me the shovel," he called down the tunnel. Lincoln handed it up, and Perry set off for the barn with Nadia on his heels.

They trudged through the snow, leaving prints from their snow shoes. What should have been a quick trip around the back of the cabin took longer because of the deep drifts. The tall doors of the barn opened inward. He dug a ramp to the floor several feet below and dropped to the icy floorboards, reaching to help Nadia.

"Watch your step. It's slippery," he warned. Perry took a look around the shadowy outbuilding. The only light was sun pouring through a window high in the wall. It was just enough illumination to see where, weeks before, Clyde MacAskill had taken a nasty fall from a ladder that was still on its side.

He glanced at the ceiling, at the narrow crack in a support beam that Clyde had been trying to repair. The old man had worried heavy snow would put a strain on the aging roof, but the structure was holding. Perry studied the crossbeams and nodded to himself, satisfied it would not come down on their heads.

"What about the snowmobile?" Nadia asked.

"Right this way." He carefully crossed to a bulky mass covered in tarp. The sleek snowmobile looked ready to go, and he thanked his lucky stars.

Perry threw a leg over the seat and turned the key in the ignition. The engine growled to life, sputtered, and threatening to expire. His eyes dropped to the gas gauge, and Nadia gnawed on her thumbnail. "Don't worry. There's a gas drum, babe."

"Thank goodness. Is this it?" Nadia moved to the metal drums and tilted one. Perry's eyebrows shot up. The drum should not have been light enough to tilt. The other barrel was on its side, the fallen ladder resting against it.

Perry hopped off the snowmobile and marched toward her. He shook one, then the other. Both empty. The ladder clattered to the cold floorboards as he knocked it aside. He kicked the downed gas drum, and it skittered across the frozen floor. Nadia's breathing rapidly accelerated. He shot a glance at her, tried to get himself under control. Despite the freezing temperatures, he had broken out into a sweat.

He wiped his brow with a shaky hand and moved back to the snowmobile to turn it off. The needle on the gas gauge remained dismally close to the E. His mouth went dry at the thought there was no way to take them to safety now.

"Can we get there on what's left in the snowmobile and refuel once we make it to town?" she asked.

Perry dejectedly shook his head.

"What are you saying, Perry?"

He looked at her with apologetic blue eyes that pierced her core with icy fear. "I'm saying we're stranded, Nadia."

～

Lincoln paced the living room, an eye on the dwindling fire. He tossed another few sticks on the pile, but the flames were barely making a dent in the cold. He shrugged into a jacket, wondering what was taking the others so long.

Daydreams of a warm hotel room washed over him. He pictured a big, soft bed and downy blankets, room service and pay-per-view. Wi-fi. Lincoln sighed dreamily. He would gladly suffer the cold a little longer to let Nadia make it there first, but he was anxious to see his companions off. The sooner Perry took Nadia to town, the sooner he could return for Lincoln.

Then, they would return to the real world, and Perry would come with them. Getting the reality TV show off the ground would give Lincoln something to do since the Landon Ashville film looked to be passing him by. Maybe it was for the best.

He wanted to call Carmen and find out if her father was willing to be their producer. Lincoln wanted to channel his creative energy into a project he believed in. Television was not his forte, but with Carmen's help, he could make his mark.

He had never considered himself relationship material, but Nadia and Perry made him want to settle down. He pictured them moving into a home together, working on the television show. But there was one thing he had to do to get the ball rolling.

He ventured into Perry's bedroom and grabbed the cellphone off the dresser, telling himself he was merely checking the time. The battery light flashed at three percent. Lincoln sighed in frustration.

"I'll make it quick," he whispered to himself. He slowly dialed the phone number to Dominic's office, ignoring the voice in the back of his head telling him he was wasting a precious resource.

Since Perry and Nadia were preparing the snowmobile for their trek to town, they would be out of the cabin by nightfall, at least. The phone could recharge at the hotel. Lincoln pressed the phone to his ear and swallowed nervously as his heart thudded in his chest. The line connected with a quiet click.

"Carmen Wilde," she answered.

"Hey! Carmen!"

"One moment, please."

Elevator music funneled through the phoneline and Lincoln stared at the device in disbelief. "She put me on hold." He paced the living room with the phone between his face and shoulder. *I should hang up. I'm gonna hang up.* A minute ticked away. He had already used up some of the precious battery power, and to hang up now would make the call in vain. Another minute passed.

"Shit, Carmen! Pick up the phone," he growled.

The phone chirped. Lincoln glanced at the screen and read the message: *Battery critically low*. His thumb hovered over the disconnect call button, but suddenly Carmen's bubbly voice returned. "Hello! This is Carmen. What can I do for you?"

"Thank God. Hey! My phone battery is low, and I was afraid the phone would die before I could speak with you. It's Lincoln."

"Oh, Dominic is back! I've been trying to reach out to you for days, but the phone kept going to voicemail," she said.

"Yeah, I'm stuck in a situation where I can't charge the phone, so we've been using it sparingly. But I really had to reach out to you before I make it back to LA. I was wondering if you could get me a meeting with your dad. I have an idea for a television show that I want to pitch."

"Normally, I wouldn't, Lincoln. People are always trying to get to my dad, but what do you have in mind?"

He scrambled to condense his show idea into a few words, knowing the battery could die at any second. "A survivor show, but not just any survivor show," he said. "We throw two teams into the wilderness, and they compete to survive anything."

"Anything?"

"With nothing but the clothes on their backs and a hunting knife."

"I hate to say it, but that's been done to death," Carmen said.

"Not like this!" he insisted. "The teams won't be made up of fitness junkies or thrill seekers. Instead, picture a bunch of rich and famous people in the wilderness. Uh, the owners of tech start-ups, popular music artists, famous brain surgeons. That kinda thing!"

"Yeah, but they won't need prize money."

"A portion of the prize could go to the charity of their choice, and the rest could go to an Average Joe teammate? I don't know! I haven't worked out all the details, but I'm sure we can come up with the proper treatment. I just need Herschel Wilde's ear."

"For you, I can make it happen."

"Oh, thank goodness!"

She giggled on the other end of the line. "I owe you one. You were so sweet on the set of *Vengeance with a Vengeance*. Your friendship helped me get over an ugly breakup, and that movie softened the effect of the nasty things the tabloids were saying about me."

"Speaking of which...There's something I need to tell you first. Nadia Marson is one of the potential producers."

"You're shitting me!" Carmen sucked in a breath. "She won't want anything to do with me! How did you even get someone like Nadia Marson to sign onto the deal?"

"We're at this survival training camp together. Don't worry. I've talked to her about you, and she's on board. I never saw the tabloid articles, but I've heard a lot about them lately. All I can say is, the differences the two of you had won't derail anything. I'm sure the rumor junkies didn't help. You should get to know Nadia. She's a real sweetheart." The phone made another funny chirping sound and powered down. "Hello? Carmen? Hello?" The line was dead.

Lincoln tossed the cellphone aside with a frustrated snarl. He went into the living room and stood on a chair near the window to peer out over the snow. He could see Nadia and Perry's feet, they were finally making their way back, and they did not look happy. He was not looking forward to telling them he had used up all the battery.

Minutes later, Nadia dropped down the snow shaft and into the living room. Perry followed. Lincoln nervously shifted his weight from one foot to the other as he waited for them to remove their coats and snow shoes.

"So? What's up with the snowmobile?" He noted the concern lines etched on Perry's forehead.

"Out of fuel. The extra container was somehow knocked over when Clyde fell from the ladder. I told Nadia it's time to call in her private helicopter."

Lincoln's heart sank to his stomach. "We can't do that."

"Why not?" Perry asked suspiciously.

"Because...I just used the last of the battery."

"You did *what?!*"

A sound like rumbling thunder rendered him mute. Perry tilted his head and listened more closely as the floor began to shake under their feet and the noise grew louder—like a jet taking off or huge waves crashing against the craggy bluff. It swelled in volume, followed by a more sinister hiss. Lincoln and Perry locked eyes with matching horror.

"What is that?" Nadia asked tensely.

"Avalanche," Perry whispered.

CHAPTER 18

The ice and snow wall struck with the force of a freight train. The cabin quaked, and the three of them were thrown to the floor like rag dolls. Nadia's shrill screams rent the air, but the sound was swallowed by the roar of the patio door as it imploded. They had nowhere to run.

"Hold onto me!" Perry shouted. Nadia gripped his fingertips, and he flailed wildly for Lincoln's hand. The white wave of snow powered its way into the house.

Perry cried out as they were pushed across the room. He tried to cover Nadia and Lincoln with his burly frame, but panic tightened his throat as he wondered if he had what it took to keep them all alive.

"No!" he gasped as the walls began to visibly shift.

The firewood stacked near the fireplace came clattering down. A log slammed into Perry, and pain exploded like fireworks in his skull. He desperately clung to his charges. He had only known these two people for a couple of weeks, but they had become his entire world.

He heard the groans of the cabin as the wind and snow hammered it. Perry knew that the odds were stacked against them, but he had to believe they would make it. As chaos reigned around them, he had to stay strong. In the swiftly fading light, he saw deep lakes of terror in both of his lovers' eyes.

"We can do this!" The strength in his voice surprised him.

Then the world went black. He knew that he was covered in snow and he was aware of a new pain emanating from the side of his head. Numbing cold swept in, bringing with it brutal silence.

"Come on, Perry! We need you." Nadia pleaded.

They were in the woods. The wolves circled the outskirts of camp. *No*, Perry thought. They had come out of the woods. The threat that had caught him unawares this situation was not one he could scare away with a gun blast. *I can't get you out of this.*

"Perry, please! Oh, my God, I love you so much. Don't do this to me. Wake up!"

She loved him, and he was in love with her. With both of them. The cold lulled him deeper into oblivion, but her sobs and whimpers pulled him back. A red-hot pain speared through his shoulder blade, completely overwhelming the dull throb in his temple. He remembered. Being in battle. Leaving someone behind. Someone else he could not save. If he gave up now, history would repeat. He had to try.

Perry weakly turned his head and opened his eyes, but he could not see. He felt his legs covered in loosely packed snow. He felt someone desperately clawing away at the pile near his shins. Groaning, he moved to extricate himself the rest of the way.

"You're alive!" Lincoln's voice hitched.

Perry gingerly sat up. A soft, warm body launched into his arms, and Nadia's tearful laughter echoed in the darkness. "You stopped breathing! We thought you were..."

"I'm okay," he promised. He kissed her forehead. He did not know how they had managed to avoid being buried in the avalanche, but they would not survive for long if he did not do something. He had to find a way out somehow.

Perry rose to his feet with a pained groan. No light penetrated the blackness. Limping to investigate the prison of ice, he let his fingers skim over hard-packed walls of snow and realized there were no more rooms, but one large cavern. They were trapped.

"Are you both alright? Is anyone hurt?"

"Fine so far, what about you?" It was Lincoln who responded.

"A bang on the head but other than that I'm good"

Perry felt his way to them. He took comfort in the touch of Lincoln's hand on his shoulder. Nadia slid between them, and they wrapped her in a hug. "I think the entire cabin is under snow," Perry said quietly.

"How long do you think we have?" Nadia whispered.

Perry shrugged. She dropped her head to his chest with a muffled sob. They had only stalled the inevitable. His eyes stung with tears at his helplessness. He cleared his throat and moved away.

"We need light," he said gruffly.

Righting the fallen escritoire, he pulled open a drawer and felt around for the flashlights Nadia had gathered up for them. When he powered on a torch, the ice cave filled with a cool, otherworldly beam that bounced off the snow. Perry stood the flashlight on end atop the escritoire and looked around.

The entrance to the kitchen was now a wall of white. They were cut off from their meagre supply of food, save for the rucksack Lincoln had packed for the snowmobile trip to town. Perry dug through the bag as his heart thudded in his chest like a slow-motion count-down.

"What are we going to do?" Nadia asked.

"There's nothing...nothing we can do but wait." He took a blanket from the sofa—one they had used the night before for their fort—and he draped it around her shoulders.

Perry felt Lincoln's hand on his back.

"Come get warm," the actor murmured.

Perry watched him take his sketchbook over to the fireplace and shove pieces of paper into the dying embers. Nadia inhaled sharply. She rushed to the sofa and pushed a hand beneath the pillows to find her notebook. More fuel for the fire. After a moment, tiny flames flickered to life, and Perry stared at it, feeling their eyes on him.

They were looking for answers and he had none. Survival was ninety percent preparedness and ten percent luck. There was no way they could have anticipated the avalanche, and their luck seemed to be running out. But he had to give them a reason to hope.

"The snow will act as an insulator," he murmured. "Like an igloo. It won't get much colder than this." Perry stared at his hands in his lap. They were large, calloused hands. Strong hands. Hands that had let them down. He took a breath and steadied his voice. "I love you too much to let myself believe this is the end."

"We're not giving up," Nadia whispered.

Nadia helped them collect the pillows and blankets that had made it through the avalanche, and they recreated the pillow fort in what was left of the living room. She had no idea how many hours passed or when night fell.

She considered that they would probably not survive and made her peace with the fact. Then, she pushed the line of thought from her mind.

Perry tucked her beneath another quilt. "Warm enough?"

She nodded and smiled. Lincoln gently stroked her hair back from her face. "So, are you ever going to tell us what you wrote in all those letters to Maria?" he asked.

"I told her that I was going through a rebellious phase, but I'm out of it now," she said.

"Oh, are you?"

His fingers whispered over her cheek and caressed her slender neck. His eyes followed the trail but traveled back to meet her gaze. Nadia nodded as she remembered her response in the woods, that some secrets were to be taken to the grave. Her adrenaline spiked once again as she confronted her own mortality. She swallowed thickly.

"This has nothing to do with rebellion. I've never loved anyone or anything the way I love you," she confessed.

Perry leaned closer. "And I've never needed anything or anyone the way I need you," he whispered. "When we get out of here, I'll prove it to you. We'll make that television show together. Everyone will know about Survive Anything."

Nadia's laugh was tinged with sadness. Lincoln's hand dipped beneath the quilt to feel her heartbeat as he added to the fantasy. "We'll be so successful that Mitch Trepan will come crawling back to beg me to make movies with him. *If* he can find me, because we'll buy a big house where the three of us can escape the pressures of fame."

She threw her head back and laughed. "And my dad will love and accept you both," she added. Her laughter tapered to a soft sigh.

Perry's expression changed. He kissed her lips with a touch of sadness. "For now, let me hold you. Let me show you how much I truly need you both," he said. Perry and Lincoln slipped beneath the covers to join her. They shed their clothes in the darkness.

Perry pulled her into his arms for a soul-stirring kiss. Then, guiding her by a fistful of hair, he led her down his chest. She nipped at his pecs and licked his rippling abs.

She groaned deep in her throat as her tongue swept over his erection, and he growled her name. Nadia took him past her lips inch by thick inch. Halfway down, she teasingly pulled away, leaving a web of spit, and his hips rose to find her mouth again. He rammed deeper, bringing tears to her eyes with the force of his passion. She gasped as she retracted.

"Yes," she begged. More. She wanted more. She wanted their passion and fury, their helplessness and hope, their fears and dreams. She wanted to give them all of hers as well.

Lincoln parted her thighs and planted his mouth at the apex of her desire. He kissed and sucked her clit, his hot, wet tongue skating circles around her engorged nub. She writhed in amazement. "I feel you throbbing," he breathed.

Nadia whimpered with desire and reached between her legs to touch herself as Perry brought her onto her side and entered her from behind. She closed her eyes as he eased inside, pressing a silky moan of bliss free.

His lips coasted over her earlobe with an airy sigh. His thighs bunched with tension. She felt Lincoln merge with him, and the three of them languidly rocked together. It was the back and forth of an ageless dance. In the frigid ice palace, the act took on new meaning.

She looked back and saw that Perry's blue eyes burned. "You're a goddess," he whispered. "I want to worship you." Nadia hitched in a breath as he penetrated deeper. His girth stretched and caressed her. The bulbous head of his cock nudged her higher, and his thrusts were accompanied with quiet grunts of exertion.

"I'm only human, but I'm yours," she groaned.

She let her head loll back on his shoulder. Perry thrust deeper, and she gripped him tighter. Ever tighter. She vigorously rubbed her throbbing clit as her pussy enveloped his hardness, and her wetness drizzled down her inner thighs.

Perry pounded in her inner grasp, hips bucking with forceful precision as Lincoln made love to him. She felt she would go up in steam from the power of their excitement. Her pussy tightened around Perry, dripping wetter with every stroke of his cock. At the same time, his mouth coursed along her skin with butterfly tenderness, and she heard the slick, wet sound of all three of their bodies colliding.

Nadia locked around him tighter, as Lincoln gasped Perry's name again in warning. Both men rammed harder and faster. She looked over her shoulder to see Perry's eyes roll back in bliss.

"Don't stop," she whimpered.

"I'll never let you go," he said. He held her tighter. All she needed was to be in his arms to be safe from all hurt, harm or danger. Nadia squeezed her eyes shut and, for a second, believed in that. She had to.

Lincoln was past the point of no return. He cried out in bliss as her core pulsed wildly and, suddenly, her orgasm unfurled, too. Nadia gasped, feeling Perry's seed explode within her in a hot gush of silky wetness that mingled with hers. They bonded in the cold darkness, knowing tomorrow was not promised, that tonight might have to be enough.

∼

L incoln slept fitfully, tossing and turning on the hardwood floor. But, whenever his lovers snuggled closer, he calmed. Their heat flowed into him like a promise of better nights to come. Nadia's slender leg pressed between his as she grinded against him in sleep. Perry's hand slid down his side and clasped his hip possessively.

He dreamed of lovemaking beneath a million stars. When he awakened, there were no stars. The flashlight had died at some point. He had no way to know how many hours had passed. The night felt eternal, and Lincoln fought panic as he considered that they were, to all intents and purposes, buried alive.

Lincoln wriggled from the pallet on the floor and ambled to the escritoire for another flashlight. As he powered on the torch, snow sprinkled from the cavern ceiling. He looked up in alarm. Would it hold? He beamed the light overhead in search of evidence of cracking or weakness, but saw none.

"Check the bucket," Perry murmured behind him.

Lincoln started and turned. "Check what?"

"For water," Perry repeated.

Lincoln absently moved to the fireplace and pulled the vase from the ashes. The snow Perry had collected the day before was now suitable drinking water. He took a sip and handed the vase to his companion, gesturing with the light. "The ceiling. I don't know if it's stable. Should we be worried?"

"What's going on with the ceiling?"

"It's...snowing."

As Perry squinted up, another dusting of snow fell. He placed the vase on the mantel and moved to the center of the room where the ice ceiling was highest. Lincoln listened for cracks in the ice but there was only an eerie silence.

Lincoln thought he heard something else, the whoop-whoop of helicopter blades. He told himself he was only hearing what he wanted to hear, but, Perry had obviously heard it too. Either there was a helicopter or they were both experiencing a matching delusion.

"We have to let them know we're down here!" Nadia stated as the realization dawned on her too.

Perry dashed to the fireplace and stared up the ceiling. "I don't see how this could be the rescue team. I pray it is, but I don't want to get your hopes up."

"Hello!" Nadia yelled. Her voice echoed through the room and raced up the chimney. "Hello! Can you hear me? Help!"

"Uh, Nadia?" Lincoln gazed up in panic as a heap more snow fell from the ceiling.

Nadia opened her mouth to scream again, but Perry wrapped his arms around her and dragged her away from the fireplace. "I want to talk to them!" she sobbed shrilly. "I have to let them know we're here!"

She wrestled to break free, thrashing wildly. Her feet came off the floor as she tried to lunge away, but Perry held tight. "Baby, baby! The whole thing could come crashing down around us," he warned. "You have to calm down."

"Wait, but she has a point," Lincoln stated. "The chimney is probably the closest to the surface. Hell, it could even be above the snow. If there's anyone up there, we have to find a way to let them know."

"Without causing another avalanche though," said Perry. Nadia slumped in his arms. He released her when he knew she would not yell again. "Quick, give me another flashlight." Perry reached for the torch and quickly dismantled it. He removed the conical reflector and raced with it to the fireplace. "Hold the light steady, Lincoln. Hurry!"

"What is it? What are you doing?" Nadia sniffed.

"The light will bounce off the reflector, right?" Lincoln suddenly realized.

"Exactly, and its dark outside so there is a chance that it may be seen, albeit a very slim chance." Perry tilted the reflector back and forth, while he shone the light. Perry crouched and peered up the chimney.

"Keep doing it anyway," said Nadia. "We have to try."

Lincoln held the light, feeling his hand tremble with nervousness. They had faced so many dangers. They had gone through so much together, and every time it seemed they had overcome, they encountered another problem. He wanted to have hope, but he was afraid.

The sound of helicopter blades came back louder near the chimney. Nadia's giddy laughter intensified as she pointed up. "They know we're here!"

CHAPTER 19

Five months later...

Perry's neighbor, Mr. Dougal, had heard the avalanche and called for help. Nadia and Lincoln went back to their respective lives and Perry returned to his, at least a semblance of it.

He was staying in a hotel while Clyde continued his convalescence at his granddaughter's house. The old man was there for a visit when Perry returned from the post office with a letter.

"What does it say?" Clyde asked.

Perry reluctantly tore open the envelope and unfolded the crisp, official-looking document. "Well, it's not much," he said after a beat, "but it'll help us start over. We can find a small house closer to town. Maybe, once we're settled in, we can even talk about re-opening Survive Anything."

With a shake of his head, Clyde rolled away in his wheelchair. "It's a crying shame. I still can't believe what Rick Feldman did to you." He gazed out the window at the snow-covered mountain in the distance. Nothing remained of the place they had called home.

"The sheriff says he'll get community service," said Perry. "I've got no bone to pick with Rick. He did what he thought he had to do to keep Empowered Survival on top, and it almost worked."

"That doesn't have to be the end of the story."

Clyde looked at him with a knowing smile. Not for the first time, Perry regretted having told him about the reality TV show idea. "We've been over this, Clyde. Herschel Wilde didn't want to invest. Besides, you need me to be here for you."

"Yeah? And what about you? You need people, too, son. Don't think I don't know that pretty little girl has been asking you to come visit with her and that actor fella." Clyde rolled his wheelchair over and positioned himself right in front of Perry. "I think you're using me as an excuse."

"Now, why would I do that?" Perry scoffed.

"I don't know, considering they're your friends. To hear you tell it," Clyde continued, "you got attacked by wolves, chased them through the forest, got snowed in together and buried under an avalanche. You don't go through stuff like that and not develop a bond. Yet, you act like they're unimportant to you."

"If I didn't know any better, I'd think you were trying to foist me off on them," Perry chuckled.

"Maybe so. Even if *you* don't want a girlfriend, I *do*," Clyde teased.

"What's that supposed to mean?"

"I've found a place. An assisted living facility."

Perry leaned back in surprise. "Go on."

"I met a lady at rehab who lives there. She told me it's a wonderful place."

Perry shook his head as he turned away. "I bet," he murmured, thinking about Nadia and Lincoln. He had not seen them since the meeting with Nadia's PR team. Although they had found a publicist to rebrand him, Lincoln had delivered the news that Herschel's production company shot down the survivor show idea. That had been that, and Perry had left well enough alone, relinquishing the dream of a future with Lincoln and Nadia because he felt Clyde needed him.

But now his old friend was telling him he was ready to move on. Perry wondered where that left him.

Clyde pulled a cigar out of his shirt pocket and clamped it between his teeth, rolling away in his wheelchair. "They seem to want you around, Perry."

"You know what they say—three's company."

"Well, now...I got the feeling you completed the picture."

"Oh, really?" Perry raised a brow, not knowing how to respond.

Clyde met his gaze and smiled. "I hear the way you talk to them on the phone."

Perry crossed his arms. "You shouldn't eavesdrop," he said lightly.

"I don't...much. I just pick up on a little here and there. Like the fact Nadia is still working to make Survive Anything a success, and Lincoln is looking for a place out here for the three of you. I don't pretend to know what's going on between you and your friends, but I think you're being dishonest with yourself if you act like there's nothing there."

"Clyde..."

The old man threw up his hands. "Now, I'm not prying, but..."

"That's extremely debatable."

"Just tell me this. Is it the girl or the guy?"

Perry ran a hand over his face and blew out a breath, chuckling quietly.

"Fine. Keep it to yourself," Clyde said with a grin. "You're not the same man you were when you came back from the war. You're ready to be a part of the world again. And, so am I. I'm moving into that assisted living facility with Margorie. I hope you support my decision because—whatever you decide to do—I support you."

Perry finally turned to the old man. He struggled with what to say. Clyde was telling him this was the end of the road for them. No more living together in a cozy log cabin in the mountains. It was not the way Perry had expected things to go. A part of him felt abandoned, another part felt freed.

"What about the business?" he asked. "I can't run the survival training camp without you. I saw firsthand how dangerous things can get without someone manning the radio while I take students out into the woods."

"I think you know what you need to do about Survive Anything. Nadia Marson never gave up on the reality TV show and neither should you. I believe in you, son."

"I never doubted that," Perry replied, smiling.

Later that evening, he sat at the hotel writing desk and stared at his cellphone. Because of his obligations to Clyde, he had given up on a relationship with his polyamorous paramours. Now, he could live anywhere, do just about anything, even if the option to make a television show was off the table. He was out of excuses to keep Nadia and Lincoln at bay. One phone call or text message would change everything.

~

L incoln was on the set of *Edge of Earth* when his phone vibrated at the precise moment Mitch Trepan said, "Action!"

He ignored the alert and clung to an artificial cliff-face as gusts of wind from an industrial fan tore at his clothes. Flurries of fake snow lashed at his frame. "I'm not gonna make it!" he yelled. "You have to let me go! You go on."

His companion clutched his wrists with a scowl of determination. "Don't give up on me now, you son of a bitch!"

"If you don't let go, we both go down!"

"Then, we both go down!" Jasper Kent put everything he had into the line.

Lincoln was deep in character, channeling the terror he had felt when he was alone and injured in the woods. It took no leap of imagination to wonder how he would react when faced with life or death. He had done that and come out a better man, just as his character would do in this film.

The fateful survival training course had prepared him for the movie, exactly as Mitch had predicted. Lincoln was still shocked he had got the part. He would never forget the day he had finally gotten around to reading the script and realized it made even more sense that Landon Ashville had written the role for him. Jasper Kent was his love interest. Audiences would go wild.

After the avalanche, Lincoln had been incapable of slotting right back into his acting career. He spent several days in the hospital recovering from dehydration and hypothermia. He spent another month on a vacation in the tropics to get over the emotional toll. He still had rough nights, but he had forced himself to return to work in LA.

Then, Mitch called about the movie, and Lincoln learned the director had not given his role to Jasper Kent. Instead, he had hired them both as leads. Apparently, that was always his intention. Now, the two of them shared the spotlight. The tension onscreen was palpable. The budding friendship between the rival actors was just as convincing. They had long since buried the hatchet.

Mitch punched the air triumphantly. "Cut!" he ordered.

Lincoln grinned and let go of the "cliff-face," dropping harmlessly to a foam pad. "How did we do?" he asked.

"Superb! You guys are dynamite together! Take a thirty-minute break. You've earned it."

"Thanks, Mitch."

Lincoln gave a short wave to his cast mates and shuffled to the sidelines to check the text. A striking young woman in a sports bra and jeans and an inviting smile on her lips wandered past. Lincoln hardly noticed.

The tabloids had gone crazy with speculation after he was rescued with the billionaire and the military vet. However, Nadia's PR team had swiftly pushed the hero narrative, placing the spotlight squarely on the kindly Mr. Dougal and the small mountain town that had hosted them.

He unlocked his phone and glanced at the screen, warming with pleasure when he saw it was Perry. "I want to see you," the text read.

Smiling, Lincoln replied, "I can do that. When are you free?"

His phone chirped again, and a selfie from Nadia filled a bubble in the group text. She looked downright edible in a black business suit, a hint of red lace peaking from the neckline. "Headed into a meeting," she replied. "Best I can do on short notice."

"Damn, I love you, Ms. Marson," he fired back.

Perry swooped into the message box: "So, about that house…"

Lincoln raised an eyebrow in surprise. The long-distance relationship still had the same fire as when the trio had been up close and personal in the woods. If anything, the distance brought them closer. However, he had been searching for a home for the three of them ever since the show idea had fallen through. He had only stopped because Nadia and Perry seemed ambivalent about moving in together.

"What changed?" he spoke into the speech-to-text app. The words fluttered across the screen. It took a moment before Perry replied.

"I think we can survive living together," he texted.

Nadia quickly answered, "OMG! Hold that thought. Continue after meeting."

"Then, we'll talk about it in person. Booking a flight to Perry now," Lincoln texted.

He shook his head, laughing softly to himself as he tabbed from the text messages to a search engine to book a flight. They could seek out a new place together. Hopefully, Nadia would be available to join them. Or they could fly out to see her, too.

After the flight was booked, he slipped his phone into his pocket and peered out over the set of the man versus nature film, filled with buoyant happiness. Were all his dreams finally about to come true?

Nadia shoved her phone into her purse and hurried to the elevator. Maria held the doors. Their lawyer slipped in behind them. "Do you think she's there yet?" her best friend asked. Nadia checked her watch.

"We're fifteen minutes early," she said. "I'm so nervous that I'm shaking. Look at me!"

"Relax. You'll do just fine."

"After all, the business plan is flawless," the lawyer assured them.

"And the two of you have talked about this on the phone and by Skype," said Maria. "It's time to meet and really get the ball rolling."

Nadia smoothed her skirt and shook her thick, lustrous hair back from her face as the elevator came to a stop. She met Maria's gaze and felt a boost of confidence. The two of them stepped out of the carriage and made their way to the meeting room.

Just outside the door, Nadia sucked in a breath and exhaled slowly. She put a hand on the doorknob, but the door opened inward, and she came face to face with the woman she was meeting. They both froze.

"Nadia?"

"Carmen," she breathed.

"My goodness! You're even prettier in person. What the hell was Jason Stratham thinking?"

Maria smoothly slipped a hand through the crook of Nadia's arm and ushered her into the room. "Clearly, he wasn't," she laughed. "Hi, I'm Maria Gonzalez. We spoke by phone. Pleasure to finally meet you, Carmen."

"Ni-nice to meet you, too. Both of you." Carmen smiled brightly. Her lawyer gestured for the group to take their seats at the large conference table in the middle of the room. They were at Dominic's office. The agent had been kind enough to allow them to use it, and he had assured them he would not breathe a word to Lincoln.

Nadia found it hard not to think about her history with Carmen Wilde, but Maria was right. She had spoken extensively with Carmen, even touching on the issue of dating Jason.

Over time, they had learned they had a lot in common. They were both the daughters of wealthy, successful men who dictated their every move. And they both wanted to prove to the world they were much more than that.

She was Nadia Marson, whether her father was Wilson Marson the oil magnate or Joe Blow the mechanic shouldn't be an issue. Nadia wanted to show her father she had a viable investment on her hands, and Carmen wanted Herschel Wilde to know she could do more than answer phones and keep schedules.

"Are you ladies ready to talk business?" Carmen asked.

Nadia shook off her bout of nerves and unsnapped her briefcase. "Absolutely, let's get this done!" she said. Maria flashed her a thumbs up. She was grateful to have her ex-housekeeper and current best friend along for this journey.

The three women were on a mission to make Survive Anything Entertainment more than the stuff of dreams. Lincoln and Perry were in the dark about what she was doing. She did not want to tell them anything until she had good news. Nadia knew that with Maria's budding entrepreneurial skills, Carmen's experience in show business and her own drive, they would not walk away from the table empty-handed.

Her relationship with her father was amicable again, and he had given up trying to hire her. He had, however, made it clear he would not sink a dime of his money into this particular business venture. So, she was teaming up with Carmen to pool their resources, and Maria was investing her entire savings. This had to work. Nadia *knew* it would work.

An hour later, Carmen sat back and squealed in delight.

"I'm sold," she said. "With the treatment you've submitted for the pilot, I'm more confident than ever. Eventually, if the ratings are high enough, we can even branch out and do other reality shows. My dad may not be investing, but he's promised me he'll mentor us along the way."

"That's more than enough for me," said Nadia.

"So, what do you say, ladies?" Maria asked. "Are we ready to incorporate?"

"I've waited for this for what seems like a lifetime," Nadia whispered. Her life had begun anew after the fateful avalanche. "Let's do this," she said excitedly.

They signed the documents knowing they were taking a leap of faith, but Nadia was unafraid.

Nadia was walking on air. She could hardly believe that she was officially a producer, and the three of them would begin work on her first project as soon as she notified Lincoln and Perry of their amazing good fortune. She raced to her car and headed straight for the airport.

～

N adia's dress slipped to the floor in a whisper as Lincoln drew her into a sultry kiss. She pressed her warm naked body against his, and Perry molded to her frame from behind. The three of them tumbled into bed together.

"So, we're moving in together?" she asked.

"If you can handle living with an unemployed ex-Navy SEAL, sure."

Nadia hid a smile, running her fingers tantalizingly over Perry's crotch. The ridge of his erection strained against the fabric, and her body tingled to feel him inside. "I've got a feeling you won't be unemployed for long," she said. "In fact, I know someone who's looking to hire."

"Mm-hmm, we'll talk about that *afterwards,*" Perry said as he nuzzled her. "I haven't seen you two in months. I just want to feel you."

"What kind of job is it? I'm intrigued," Lincoln murmured, groaning as she clutched his erection in hand. She pulled his hard-on through the opening of his briefs and leaned down to wrap her lips around him. Her thick, black hair cascaded around her face, and Perry laced his fingers through it and brought her to his lips to kiss the taste of Lincoln from her tongue.

"You'll never guess…"

"I give up," Perry replied, rolling on top of her.

She lost her train of thought as the sex got steamier, and he stole her ability to speak. The trio tangled beneath the sheets together. Her ecstasy climbed higher and higher. Only Perry and Lincoln could do this to her.

Their connection had been forged in snow and ice and had survived the worst that life could throw at them. Not only did Nadia want Lincoln and Perry to move in with her, but she wanted their relationship to be set in stone. They were in love. They were about to be business partners. The commitment was real.

And she would show them the time was now.

An hour later, she tossed back the covers and stared up at the ceiling with a satisfied smile. Lincoln turned on his side and grinned down at her as Perry rose from between her legs with a satisfied sigh.

"About that job," she said.

"I'm listening."

Nadia told them about Survive Anything Entertainment. She told them how Carmen Wilde and Maria had joined forces with her to make the business a reality, and the room went silent. She studied their faces, trying to gauge how they felt. Lincoln looked stunned. Perry's expression was guarded. "Scared?" she asked quietly.

Lincoln responded, "More like, ready for another adventure..."

Perry shook his head and sat up, and Nadia's spirits sank. If he was not on board, then all of this had been for nothing. He glanced over his shoulder with a crooked smile. "I told you we could survive anything together. I'm in."

STAY INFORMED ABOUT NEW RELEASES FROM NICOLE STEWART!

Visit the link below to **sign up to get list exclusive discounts, news about new releases, and the opportunity to be a VIP reviewer and get all my books for FREE for life!**

http://beechwoodpublishing.com/nicolestewartfans

I promise that this is not a spam list.

Made in the USA
Columbia, SC
15 December 2021

51657180R00114